Against the Clock

A Collection of Stories and Poems, written to raise funds on behalf of The Alzheimer's Society

Publication arranged by Root Creations.
A Leaf Books Ltd Imprint

First published in 2007

www.leafbooks.co.uk

Leaf Books Ltd.
GTi Suite,
Valleys Innovation Centre,
Navigation Park,
Abercynon,
CF45 4SN

Printed by Jem
www.jem.co.uk

ISBN (paperback) ISBN no 978-1-905599-41-7

Edited by Paul Zealand

Cover Design by Steve Upham

On Friday 12th October 2007, sixteen members of The Grail Internet writing group – plus one couple's two children – spent many of the hours between noon and midnight writing as many stories and poems as possible, based on 100 prompts posted that morning.

This followed a period of sponsor-seeking via the new-fangled ('Just Giving' websites)
and the old-fashioned (pen and paper) methods that ultimately raised over £3,000 in donations for this year's selected charity, The Alzheimer's Society.

Full information on the effects of Alzheimer's Disease, and other forms of dementia, is available on the charity's website at: http://www.alzheimers.org.uk/site/index.php

This Collection, chosen from the 269 stories and poems written in that 12-hour writing marathon, is dedicated to all those lost to, or suffering from, Alzheimer's Disease and other forms of dementia. The prompts that inspired the stories and poems are indicated, unless they are the same as the title.

To personalise the project, the named individuals below were nominated by the writers:

Doris Hodkinson: 1900-1983 (Gran)
Ellen Fredrika Clausson: 1895-1978 (Mia's Mormor, Mutti)
Peter Morris: 1930-2006 (Emma's Daddy)
Harry Weekes: 16 May 1929-still fighting (Papa)
Rakel Smith: 1898-1975 (grandmother)
Karin Johnsen: 1930-2006 (mother)
Norman Davies: 1919-2004 (father)
Moira Redmond: 1928-2006 (my dear friend)
Lucia Todesco: 1932-2002 (mother)
Wendy Swingler: no dates available (cousin)
Doreen Marks: 1917-2007 (mother, nana and great nana)
Dr. Denys Charles L'Estrange Burges: 1928-2005

Index

Paul Zealand

Have Drum, Will Travel

Prompt: The way home

The stench still gets to me, even after . . . but I've lost track of time. It must be a week at least. The hard boards under me are slick with old sweat and shit. A fellow passenger on my right groans before vomiting, but the stillness of the man on my left indicates death. My last sane memory is of the Monday night African drum class in safe, white, middle-class Harrogate. Maybe it was the patronising attitude that got me here, with jokes about tub-thumpers and my favourite: 'What do you call a guy who hangs around with musicians? A drummer!' Oh har har, my ribs are aching! But not from humour, from the kicks of crew members unimpressed by my explanations.

I should never have bought that djembe off eBay. 'Genuine Gambian-made, 19th Century djembe, a real collector's piece.' I put in a joke bid of a fiver and got the damn thing.

So from lesson one I pounded out rhythms like a natural, way beyond the level of the class. The teacher was impressed to the point of being seriously pissed at me.

'Where did you find that drum?' she asked, staring at my hands with hungry eyes.

'eBay.'

'Be careful with it. Some of these old drums are . . . unusual to say the least. Let me see the design–'

No chance! I'd told her 'hands off' then, left her in no doubt what I thought and set off on a rolling solo that had her recoiling, wide-eyed. I caught a whiff of her fear. How did she know?

That night I dreamed myself into the middle of a beaten

earth clearing, hammering out my rhythms with a dozen or so others, surrounded by swaying dancers, all of us too high on the music to notice the visitors.

Now I'm chained in a ship's hold en-route – I reckon – for America. Still, when I get there somebody will surely listen to me and show me the way home.

Post Mortem

Prompt: Died in the wool

I lean forward into the body cavity. Devoid of most organs, there is plenty of space and opportunity to examine the kidneys, peritoneum and all-important lymph nodes. Cause of death is a given, but my remit is to determine age, sex – not as easy as you might think, under these circumstances – state of nutrition and extent of any morbid conditions.

The kidneys are beautiful. Smooth and glistening, robed in greasy fat from which they consent to be teased by my gentle fingers. They are in perfect health.

Next, the peritoneum, lining the abdominal cavity. A pearlescent pink, there is nothing wrong here beyond a few small petechial hemorrhages, courtesy of the state of mind and body at death.

Within the chest is disaster. The pleura rough and cheesy with tuberculosis, the lymph nodes fat with disease. I incise downstream of the infection, confirming the bacilli have spread far enough to infect the whole body.

'I'm sorry.' I turn to the man next to me, who peers past at close range, worry giving him myopia.

'What? Can't I take her home? For the family?'

'No. Sorry. I have to condemn the carcass. This lamb is unfit for human consumption.'

A Hand Me Down

Prompt: Grandpa's chair

Oak-framed, straight-backed and with a wicker seat, the chair's comfort belies its Spartan design and materials. It looks out of place in this old allotment shed, but at least is still in use – unlike so many unwanted artefacts in this throwaway society of ours. I mean, the local tip is the first port of call for anybody with a credit card deciding on a home makeover.

My Gran told me this chair was one of a set of eight, used as dining chairs for the forty years of her marriage to Granddad. When he died, Gran moved in with us and her house and furniture had to go.

Dad kept this chair, the only one with armrests. Granddad's special, head-of-the-table chair. I can see him now. Carving the Christmas turkey, refusing to wear a paper hat but with eyes twinkling hard, like nativity stars. It was easier to concentrate on those older memories. The new ones are too raw.

'It'll go in my shed, a bit of comfort for when I need a rest.' Dad said, trying to lighten the mood of the house clearance. 'Allotments are hard work, you know . . .'

Of course we knew. He was entitled to take it easy after a hard morning rotovating stiff, compacted soil or an evening hoeing out the weeds from the planted rows. It didn't stop us making fun though. Dad on the skive, a shed full of beer, a newspaper and a shelf of his beloved Western novels. A haven away from his female-dominated, sonless home.

Until he died.

Now the allotment will go back to the society and the hard-faced buzzard on the next plot has eyes on the shed. He makes me want to torch it. I pop a can of Dad's warm

A Night Out

Prompt: Two men down

Lisa heard the beat of footsteps behind her. A second set joined in, a low laugh and murmured words indicating the two men knew one another.

Tonight was her first time out alone, but she was confident of handling these two. Without her mentor, Christopher.

But then his instructions echoed in her head.

Pick a loner.

Well, she *had*, but the sad git found a mate. The breeze carried their scent – a mix of aftershave, tobacco smoke, beer and lust – but the underlying essence made her reckless. So what if there were two of them? She was ready.

'Hey boys. Fine night, isn't it? Like my outfit?'

Lisa waggled the fairy wand, the silver star at its tip glinting in the glow from the streetlights. The short, sequined skirt she wore revealed most of her fishnets and the body-hugging basque was minimal.

'Oh, come on now. Am I not the fairy godmother? Let me take a closer look at you.'

One of them stepped forward, offered a hipflask. 'Fancy a drink?'

Lisa smelled cheap vodka. Something else. A mixer?

'Go on then.' She took the flask and drank. 'Good stuff. Your turn?'

'I don't think so, sweetheart.'

His face swam before Lisa's eyes. A flash of awareness hit her. The easiest way to a shag was a date rape drug. She had laughed with the others at the idea. As if they would fall for it! She swayed, grabbing at damp brickwork for support, before sliding to the pavement.

'You stupid, arrogant, unreasonable bitch!' Christopher's spittle rained on Lisa's bowed head. 'Why do you think we have a mentor system? If it wasn't for the good of the clan, I'd've let them shag some sense into you.'

'I'm sorry–'

'"Sorry" doesn't cut it! What am I going to do with you?'

Lisa looked up, full of regret and love. He had looked out for her.

'Have you eaten?'

'No.'

'Well, come on then.' He lifted one man's head clear of the ground, opened the exposed throat with a slash of iron-hard fingernail. 'This one's still breathing.'

Rumbled
Prompt: Motorway

I knew there was a problem when I started thinking it was okay to try the long blink.
Just dropping the lids for a little while longer than normal, to soothe my gritty, aching eyes. At night, contacts lenses don't contribute to road safety, they generate flares from the headlights, refracting sharp photons every which way into my brain and turning the clear windscreen into an obstructive hell of smears and streak. All that out-staring of lights and concentration to focus beyond the glass takes its toll, but at least it keeps me awake.

The worst times are in daylight. Like now. Benign driving conditions, allowing autopilot to kick in, my mind to wander. I'm stuck behind a lorry. Well, I *could* overtake, but it's easier to relax a bit and pootle along at a steady sixty until I can leave the motorway. Part of the problem is that I am sick to death of this road. One hundred and twenty seven miles a day, five days a week, for twenty years to date. I know every foot of tarmac, have experienced every possible weather condition and can list the average roadkill toll by species – badgers have taken over from foxes this year, but no rabbits so far.

The iPod blasts Fallout Boy, but the music doesn't register and I know that is the first symptom. I open the driver's side window, but the road racket and filthy spray drifting back from the lorry ahead puts paid to that idea. The car heater is set on maximum cool, the fans blowing into my face and dehydrating my lenses so they begin to lift clear.

Twenty miles to go. A service station is a mile distant, but I need to get home. What's the point in forcing crap, expensive coffee down if the time for the last of the journey is doubled?

A sense of imbalance makes me jerk the wheel left, getting me out of the middle lane just as an SUV flashes past with a blast of horn.

This is good. Adrenaline surges and for a short time I am as alert and perky as a Red Bull addict.

The lorry in front transforms. The loading platform hanging low at the back is now a wide, grinning mouth. Eyes pop open in a vast, square face and wink at me. I look away, and then back. Now it is laughing, but not unkindly. My friend the lorry speaks inside my head, saying a long blink is fine, that nobody will know and in any event he will look after me. I close my eyes, but keep the steering wheel centred. As long as I'm careful, I know I can do this to a count of ten at first, then twenty. I feel so much better now, will arrive home fresh and able to enjoy my evening.

At seventeen, a grinding racket drags me back and I flail at the steering wheel, grabbing the smooth plastic and jerking away from the roadside rumble strip.

I straighten up the car and drift back onto the shoulder, slowing to a stop and parking. The lorry is just a lorry, disappearing into the murk.

That is three times in the last two weeks. My heart beats fit to burst and I know I will be okay now, will drive home the rest of the way as awake as anyone. I have two job applications in. Either will do, but will I manage it in time.

Too Many Meetings

Prompt: Give me a break

The bell rang.

'God *damn* it. Not already!' Matthew threw down the hoe, flattening a row of seedlings, then turned and stamped away from the garden. His garden!

As if there wasn't enough to do with the digging and weeding and hoeing; general odd-job maintenance work and housekeeping chores without these six interruptions a day. I mean, he did most of the work around here anyway, so should be excused these tiresome meetings.

'About time I stood up for my rights,' he murmured, a little too loudly for the organisational ethos, before adopting a humble demeanour to enter the cold, airy space of the main building.

Afterwards, Matthew was summoned to the office of the man he called The Boss.

'Matthew, it grieves me to realise you are unhappy here. It there anything I can do to help?'

'Well, you could excuse me the two afternoon meetings, for a start. I'd have time to do my work properly then.'

The neat, grey-haired man in the dark robe shook his head. 'Then you will be missing the point of being one of us, Matthew. Besides, we call our six daily gatherings the "prayers" or "offices", not "meetings". Also, I am "Father Abbot" not "The Boss" and you are a lay brother who I fear will never become a monk.'

A Story Update

Prompt: A time to cull

Rool hunted the forest, wary for the scent of the enemy. His mother died protecting him, long after his father was killed, leaving him the last adult of a once great tribe that roamed the vast forest at will, fearing no man or beast.

Until the hunter returned.

All he had left was his name, Rool, 'Bright Eye' in the old language, spoken now by none save him, then only in his mind. The loneliness was at times so crushing, Rool felt he might be better off dead, but hunger was a stronger imperative than fear or despair and today it gnawed at his belly like never before.

Prey was now bold and more numerous. The deer filled the forest, strong males guarding the vulnerable, more at risk from their own squabbles than any predator. As a result, Rool was forced to eat insects, slugs and the occasional mouse, shamed by his inability to live as the leader of his tribe of one.

This day Rool roamed further than ever before, entering territory shunned even by his father when he was the tribe's last leader. There he found food.

A dead fawn lay in a small clearing. Nothing moved in the open space except a few sun-scattered shadows, yet Rool knew the food was a trap. A realisation he no longer cared combined with the wonderful scent of fresh meat to send him trotting into the clearing.

Rool's heart nearly failed at the flash of red to his left, confirming the worst fears of his cursed tribe, hunted on this day to extinction by a mad beast that knew no mercy.

Enough, thought Rool. I shall face it. He stood his ground over the carcass and growled as the hooded figure advanced, dressed all in red, wielding the woodcutter's axe.

'For my grandmother,' it said.

The Boss is Always Right
Prompt: Death of an Antichrist

'I leave you in charge for five minutes and . . .'

'With respect, it was a sight longer than that!' Luke answered with more asperity than usual, surprising himself.

The old man glared at his junior. 'Don't presume to interrupt me. If you want to succeed here you will have to work on your attitude.'

'While yours is fine, is it? I mean, you don't see a certain inconsistency in the way you apportion blame, yet fail to take any responsibility for the mess you left the place in?'

'How *dare* you!'

Ancient or not, he was still a formidable presence when angry. Thunder crashed and the Host muttered within its ranks, glaring at Luke. Massive, noble head, white-haired and with a luxuriant beard curling down his chest, if only Blake had known how close he was at depicting the leader.

'I slaved away on my own to make this place what it is ...'

'Yes, before swanning off on other projects and leaving the boy in charge.'

'My son was let down – by you, most of all. So don't try to blame him. His time will come again.'

'Not if I can help it,' Luke muttered, knowing the old man would not hear. Already he was looking tired and confused, wondering why he was arguing. Luke tried reason.

'Look, why don't you just hand over to me and enjoy your retirement. We can manage and maybe . . .' It was the wrong move. Too soon.

'Oh yes. And look at the mess you have made of it so far? I come back to find I still have a monopoly, yet nobody can agree on anything. The basic principles are twisted, the strong prey on the weak, the weak take their revenge in my name–'

'So it has ever been.'

'Well it stops now. Begone Lucifer, I cast you out. Henceforth, you are dead to me.'

Su Laws Baccino

Palaces in the Air

Prompt: Another sleepless night

clouds travel magically building
around imagined scaffolding
against houses castles homes
etched in a vast blue sky
where the wind often
visits disturbs
the vision
wrecks all
blows

Tranquil Te-di-um

Prompt: Killing time

Fans
spin,
cooling
sultry air
on old veranda.
Grandpa rocks gently in his chair,
smoke spirals from ancient pipe. Grandma knits. Cat
stretches.

Hanging Around

Prompt: A photograph of her

Slightly squiff on the wall, my formidable
Aunt Eliza hangs precariously over a cabinet;
it's full of her junk – trinkets and stuff I don't like –
heirlooms that have to stay. She's long gone,
but it's her stare, you see; with her China blue eyes,
she watches me. From an experienced face
full of craters and ditches, her frown is alive,
it bores into me; her lips sometimes curl,
make the mole – the one that sprouts the hair – twitch.
She's dead, but she's there, and I'm aware
of the smell of her clothes, mothballs; the sound
of her rasping tongue, the hiss as she sucks
air through the gaps in her teeth. Wrinkled
and worn she stares down from a stained leather
frame – another relic, it too as old as the hills.

Timeshare

Prompt: The way home

Sunday evening. Weekend now over,
queues of slow-moving, reluctant
cars, Dads crossing town en route.
The return – for the week – of their shared children
to the other
half of wrecked
bliss, their
Mum.

Springing
Prompt: Ripples of Life

From out of cold earth
spring daffodils, crocuses,
narcissi; new born
lambs, watched by mother, skip in
fields now that Spring is here.

Windsurfers fly up
over swimmers, jet-skiers
laughing and playing
below. Gulls wait for picnic
scraps. Mum tends to the sunburn.

Autumn's heavy touch
makes itself felt this morning.
Warm breath on cold panes,
a filter to the outside
world, at snail's pace dissipates.

Drifting, driven by
icy north wind covers all,
hushes, except rasp
of tyres on virgin snow, soft
sound of flakes on closed windows.

Enduring
Prompt: Grandpa's chair

By the window it has pride of place
next to the new television
close to the radiator
brushed by the long curtains
over the dog's box.
The owner's missing
Grandpa's long gone
his cushion
squashed flat –
warm.

Dark Links
Prompt: Seventeen letters and one reply

Postman's late this morning, his red bike's
still there, hidden in the hedgerow,
ready to propel him up
and down roads, in and out
of driveways, paths, lanes.
Villagers lean
on gates –
wait.

Innocent in Stockwell
Prompt: Report, as in gunshot

I queue with friends, willing the bus to arrive;
it chugs down the hill, ready to carry me on.
An innocent in waiting – if only I'd known.
The bus is full, but at least I'm on.
It's moving so slow, I urge it forward;
time is precious – I check my watch.
tick tock tick tock
The underground station's now in sight,
the bus stops, but the rush hour traffic continues on.
I pick up a paper on my way to the platform.
tick tock tick tock
Moving onto the escalator with the commuting crowd
I see my train waiting at the platform below.
I take a step left and run two at a time.
tick tock tick tock
I've made it . . . just. I sigh and smile with relief
as I dive into a seat. I'll not be late today.
bang bang bang bang bang bang bang
Seven times in my head, and then,
bang
once in my shoulder for good measure.
I'm surely dead, but my watch ticks on.
tick tock tick tock

The Unfinished Dress

Prompt: Tight red dress

Great Grandma wore a doily on her head.
I was never quite sure
if it was meant to be there.
Was it that crocheted piece
from the back of her chair
or was it, perhaps, one of those caps
like Queen Victoria used to wear.
A strange old bird,
short and square,
no real shape,
her clothes black, brown, or grey.
Mid-Summer, mid-Winter
she wore long-sleeved woolly tops.
Voluminous ankle-length skirts
that caught frequently on concertinaed
lisle stockings stuffed tight into wooden clogs;
in which she walked with a clomp,
lifting her feet high with every step
as if frightened of missing the ground.
Wrapped around her ample frame,
hip to hip, an apron with a pocket,
out of which peeped a crochet hook
and a ball of bright red cotton.
She said she was making me a dress.
Great Grandma laughed a lot, reached crescendos
so great, so loud, I sometimes
thought her house would fall down.

More than a Baptism - 1921
Prompt: Guilt

'Come on lad, you're late, they're all waiting for you.'

Fred passed his hands over his dripping suit. Then he followed Jack, his mate, along the gorse-lined shingle path towards the church, its blue-grey stone coruscating in the brilliant sun; away from the troubled group he'd been working with, and the crystal white sheets spread on the ground.

Water now dripped from every piece of Fred's clothing and even his new shoes, bought for the occasion, felt soggy, boat-like, and they squeaked with every step. He stank. He turned to Jack, 'Does Phoebe know?'

Fred was a proud father; he'd looked forward to his son's baptism, but right then, all he wanted to do was go home. He paused at the church door, briefly contemplating just that, wondering if he dare. Then he caught sight of Phoebe's shocked expression. She had obviously been told, but did she know everything? The church organ interrupted his thoughts, beckoned them in.

'It's all right. They've told the Vicar. He'll get it over and done with quickly,' whispered Phoebe, pulling him to her side. His clothes left a big wet, dirty patch on her new outfit, the one she'd been sewing for weeks. Fred shook as he crossed the threshold into God's place. The church was full. Noticeable gasps followed them down the aisle as guests noticed Fred's sodden state. He looked down at the cold stones beneath his feet and wished they would open up.

A few minutes earlier Fred had been hanging upside down on the end of a rope, deep in the bowels of the local earth, down a well. First he found the baby – Tom – dirty, but surprisingly dry. Fred wept. The second lowering was more difficult. The child's mother had fallen awkwardly and he had to move her body away from the uneven brick walls of the shaft. In the lonely deep of the pub garden, in the pitch, he ran his hands over every part of her body – each move creating an echo in the shaft, in sinister waters disturbed for the first time in years; it was the only way of deciding how to free her. He was rescuing from a tomb.

In the church Fred went through the motions, helped by Phoebe, but he heard little of what was said, instead he recalled the last time he fondled Kate. He laughed when she told him Tom was his son. Laughed, told her not to be silly. Condemned her to a life of shame. She chose this terrible end.

The service over, Fred and Phoebe retraced their steps down the lane, on their way to the family gathering. As they passed the well at the bottom of the pub garden, a man shouted angrily as he helped load two coffins onto the waiting horse-drawn hearse – one horribly small,

'This is your fault, Fred Swanscombe. You did this!'

Fred paused in his stride – then walked on. Somebody else knew.

Mia Hopkins

A Small Life
Prompt: Walking with Wordsworth

If there's only sky and silence
On the other side, then I shall not
Miss those things that poets eulogise:
No crowd of golden daffodils,

No little fly in summer's play,
No red, red roses, newly sprung,
No crimson of my lover's lips,
But this:

The splutter of a percolator,
Smells of coffee beans in brew,
Tails smattering 'gainst floorboards,
Awaiting morning walks off leads.

Boys bickering 'bout nothing
In the backseat of my car,
How my house whispers solitary
Silence when they're away at school.

Your hand in mine that fits
Just right, the way you read
My thoughts, and yet
Surprise me with your own.

No, I will not walk
With Wordsworth
But hope to remember
A small life well lived.

Alien

Prompt: Life on Mars

If I came from Mars,
I'd see with clarity
why I stand outside
the circle, while those inside,
linked by chink-less chains,
understand something
fundamental
that I'm not privy to.

They hold such secrets
close inside; a sense
of their belonging.
Or is it just
their language, one
I speak a little of
but do not fully
understand.

From a Martian viewpoint,
the distant, far away visions
cast through rose-tainted clouds,
would make me giggle
at their peculiarities
and not so wholly
feel like now,
a foreigner.

Having Your Own

Prompt: Tiny little feet

The baby gurgles in my arms, purses her mouth and slowly, imperceptibly, her eyes close. She is light in my arms, as light as air, and just as fresh. Underneath the pink swaddling blanket, tiny feet move against my arm as they fall into slumber.

I rock, in a swaying motion, from foot to foot, as slow as branches in a warm summer breeze.

'She likes you,' says the mother, Jane, sitting at the table.

I've offered to hold the baby whilst she eats, remembering all too well how stressful lunch parties were when my children were babies.

Jane scoops another bite into her mouth, chews as if this meal is a race against time, and swallows. 'It's nice to use both hands to eat,' she adds, and sips from a glass of red wine.

My husband is staring at me, his eyes narrowed in a question. I pretend not to notice, instead lean in towards the baby and whisper, 'Play along, sweet thing.'

'How old are yours now?' someone asks me.

'Too old to cuddle. Five and seven, and boys too. Not allowed to kiss them any more.'

To prove my point I land a whisper of a kiss on her forehead.

'Broody?' Jane asks me, grinning.

'And how!' I smile down at the baby.

My husband gasps for air; his eyes bulge, fishlike.

I lean in again, let scents of talcum powder and baby newness fill my nostrils.

'If we keep this up,' I say so only she can hear, 'I may get that horse after all.'

Something On Her Mind

Prompt: Malignant Tendencies

There must have been a look on her face, a look of consternation, because the nurse at the check-in desk said, 'Is there something on your mind?'

Victoria laughed. 'Yes. Something big. And it keeps growing.'

The nurse, seemingly used to such behaviour, nodded. 'Of course. Well, let's see if we can get rid of that, then.'

The head clamp had been fitted at an earlier visit. It was a contraption of metal with padding where it held the skull, and on the screws that would make sure she could not move. It made sense to her – the doc wouldn't want any movement whilst he dug into her brain for the impostor – but it made her look a monster. She'd joked about that, and about the titanium screws that would hold her head together afterwards. She'd imagined going through the airport security check and have guns drawn on her as the machine went off. Even her jokes had malignant tendencies; they tended to spread.

'It's an oligodendroglioma,' she'd told her brother. 'Such a pretty name. Like a flower . . . Hydrangea, Digitalis purpurea, Astrantia . . . Oligodendroglioma.'

He'd smiled at her then; for a second the 'you-have-cancer' look left his eyes. 'It's a bastard to say, though.'

'They should give brain tumours nasty names, in grades. Mine, a not-so-bad one, should be a Gaddafi, or an Amin. And the really nasty one – the Glioblastoma – should be called a Hitler.'

He'd patted her head. 'How's Gaddafi today?'

'A pain in the neck.'

The neurosurgeon came to talk to her whilst they shaved the part of her head that gave access to the Temporal Lobe. He had reassuringly bad bedside manners. Surgeons should be arrogant shits with sharp elbows; it was only fitting. She'd have thought twice about letting him into her head, had he been nice.

'Whilst you're in there,' she asked, 'could you make me less bitchy? Get rid of my PMT?'

There was not even a flicker of a smile on his lips. Perhaps, he'd heard it before. He shook his head. 'If I could, I'd have operated on my wife years ago.'

Yes, she thought, he would do.

Soon, she was put under and as she woke, a nurse appeared; a green mummy with vivid blue eyes visible above the mask. 'We've started de-bulking,' she said.

Victoria knew what it meant. Her growth, her uninvited visitor, lived next to the speech centre. She'd laughed at that when she first found out, and told all her friends that she hosted a foreign language student.

Now, it was time for the doctor to see how far he could cut without harming the healthy cells that controlled her speech.

The nurse held up a picture. 'Tell me what you see.'

'A welly,' Victoria said.

'You mean a boot?'

Hell, Victoria thought, this was complicated. American, not English.

Another picture moved in front of her.

'A lorry.'

'Truck.'

'A pushchair.'

'Stroller.'

'A . . . banana? Boat?'

'Bicycle.' The nurse corrected her and looked above her head. 'Word salad,' she added.

Word salad, the neurologist's term for the speech centre losing control.

A voice said, 'OK, let her go. I've got most of it.'

As she sunk into nothingness again, she wondered if it would leave a hole. And if she might miss it from that space. It had excused her behaviour for so long.

Thoughts at Dawn

Prompt: Skin seeking skin

Elbows, knees, all bones,
knuckles, sinew, nudge
then creep into
the hollow my body
leaves in slumber.

I fold, envelope you,
inhale
scents of mud,
sand and caterpillars
from the hair tickling
my cheek. I dream

of how once, I protected
you in this way,
and wished it to last
forever, frightened
it would not,

that when grown up,
your skin would
not seek mine
when spiders come
at night.

As dawn breaks,
enlightening, my aim
clear; motherhood
is to carry
a child until
you're not needed
any more.

Wrapped Up
Prompt: The curse

The wrapping paper shines with silver drops on white. I measure the gift on it to make sure it fits just right.

Summer has arrived; the children have one more day of school before they are off to my soon-to-be ex-husband, and her. The soon-to-be new wife. It's her thirtieth birthday, I've been ordered to buy gifts from the children.

'I need her to know that they love her,' he said over the phone, then hesitating before he corrected himself. 'Well, not love . . . accept.'

But they're not interested, my children.

'She lies by the pool with her boobs out,' says one.

'Won't let us wake daddy before nine,' says the other.

'I'm sure you'll like her once you get to know her,' says I.

That's what I have to say. She's a part of their future; there is nothing I can do about it. Except this.

I wipe a bead of sweat from my forehead and slide the scissors over the ribbon. It
contracts into a tight curl. A baby blue curl. For a moment, I'm taken back to the birth of my first-born, a boy, like his father wanted. Exactly how it was supposed to be. The thought perishes like the sweat that bothers my brow. Can't think like that any more. The scissors nick my thumb as they slide over the ribbon; it breaks. I lick the blood, apply a plaster and start again.

That's what he wanted, to start again. She's thirty. I'm forty-five, leftovers, remains on a plate he ate from. The gifts are lovely, bought for their new home. The home with a pool, and a tennis court. He tells me over the phone, every so often, what he plans to do with it, that he is putting in planning for an orangery.

I listen, encourage, and he tells me how happy he is that

I'm taking it this way.

'I thought you'd make it impossible for us,' he says, 'you're being so mature about it.'

Mature. I taste the word. Unless you are a fruit, a bottle of wine, or a slab of cheese, maturity is over-rated.

So I wrap the presents, make them look nice. I want her to say, 'Look, I can barely bring myself to open these, they're so pretty.'

Because he will know who it was that stood in the summer heat, wrapping presents. And he'll wonder why.

I have friends who are first wives, discarded like me.

'I'll take him to the cleaners,' they say with scarred voices, and eyes full of betrayal.

I won't. Instead, I've placed a curse on their home: I'll be the best first wife ever.

His favourite homemade jam is ready to travel, in jars with a checked cloth on top. I've packed brochures of orangeries with post-it notes on the pages he will like. A note is paper-clipped to the pile. 'Call me if you need help.'

An angry first wife cements the new relationship, makes it the two of them against her. But someone like me . . . She won't understand why he wants *my* jam on his toast, why he wants *my* children on the holidays, why he asks *me* for advice on what to do with their house.

With a final flick of the scissors the ribbon curls. Waves of contentment come over me as I see how beautiful her gifts are.

She'll get all wrapped up in that.

The Birch Family
Sharon

Morning Sun

Red striations
Orange glow
Waving green grass
In a little light blow
New earth is beginning
New life day
All is quiet
Soothing away
Lithe wispy gray
Peaceful hope
Looks out at sea
Bright beginnings
Beckoning me

Mum's Gone to Iceland

'Mum's gone to Iceland.'

She looked me up and down, mouth curled and eyes flashing with a disregard that belongs to those kids of a certain age.

'When will she back?'

'When she's ready, s'pose.' She leant against the door frame, arms crossed with matriarchal authority.

'When did she go?'

'A bit ago.'

I could tell I wasn't going to get much more from her. A baby cried from inside.

'Who's that?' I had to ask.

'Amelia.' With that look in her eyes and the tone of her voice, I felt for her. She knew she was beaten, that it was done. She moved away from the entrance. 'You'd better come in then.'

I smiled, knowing she wouldn't return it but I wanted to be friendly. As expected, I received her scowl. The uniform policeman followed. At least he took off his helmet.

Entering the eleventh floor property, I saw the struggle this young girl was having. Three children under ten sat quiet on the grubby cloth settee. Sallow eyes followed me as I went from room to room. They knew what I was there for. I wasn't so sure, but I could guess by the smell coming from the padlocked door.

'Shelley, you have to let us in there.'

'No, I don't!' Tears coursed down her dirty face. I wanted to hug her, make it all right, but I knew what I must do first.

'Shelley, if you don't let us in, this policeman will have to

break the door down.
We don't want to scare the little ones. Why don't you open the lock.'

'NO,' she screamed, red-faced, defiant.

'There isn't a choice.' I reached out to her, and took her hand in mine, and held it tight. I looked at her, straight in the eye. I had to make her trust me. 'I promise, I will do my very best to help, all of you. I know this is a very hard thing but I'll help you.' Locking eyes, I promised again.

'You can't,' she sobbed. Her wild face, filled with grief, knew what would happen next. She'd been here before, as the eldest.

But we both knew this time was different.

As she keyed the lock open, she said, 'I had to put the padlock on, to stop the others from coming in. I told them she was sleeping.'

And there laid her mother, on the unmade double bed. A small empty brown bottle by her side once held the prescription tranquilisers for her postnatal depression. It wasn't enough to keep her from another overdose. This time was fatal.

Shelley had done her best to keep the family together, but after so many failed
appointments and the children absent from school, there had to be a problem.

And now we had to find a permanent foster home for five children aged twelve years to six months. Together, as I promised.

A Time to Cull

At eight months pregnant, Denise felt fat. She looked fat, felt fat, and had never felt more unattractive. If it wasn't for Ted telling her how much he loved her, she'd have a right downer. Ted was a fantastic father to Sally and little Eddie; better than their own had been, but she didn't want to remember that.

'I'll take them camping this weekend,' he offered when she complained of how tired she was. 'There's a fair in Scarborough. They'll love it.'

A weekend to herself; it was a dream – and he was a dream.

Hot after a bath, it was too early for bed and the kids were due to ring at eight. With the latest chick flick film, and some special chocolate, she'd set herself up for the night.

Rooting through the piles of kids DVDs, music CDs and other kiddie junk, she found 'Saddle Sore'. Intrigued, she inserted the disc. It looked like a fake copy. She hoped it wasn't porn, the type Ted brought back from the pub, cheap at four quid a time. She'd not heard of this one.

Tacky music played. She watched, shocked when she saw Ted come on screen. He was standing in the garden and waving at the camera. He pretended to strip and she recognised his newish swimming trunks, bought for the summer holiday they couldn't take because of her unexpected pregnancy.

He turned and mooned. Spinning back round, he laughed and pulled out his penis, masturbating to the camera as the person recording his actions sang out a giggle. Ice trickled down Denise's back and the screen jolted, flicking to their bedroom. A female lay on her back, dressed in black stockings and suspenders, with legs apart. She was fully shaved. Denise closed her eyes, hot rage twisting knots inside her. Unable to stop the vomit, she fell forward to the floor. The first crack of pain ripped across her hard belly and she clutched her stomach. Mocking laughter began on screen and she looked up to see the girl standing close to the camera, rubbing her small, pubescent breasts against Ted's groin as he recorded the action. Retching rancid bile, her waters broke.

She ran to the gun cupboard and pulled out Ted's shotgun. Shaking, she loaded it. History had a habit of repeating itself; a cliché she thought had been broken. It hadn't.

Denise laid on her thirteen year old daughter's bed. Images of Sally and Ted flashed in front of her and also on the screen downstairs. Denise gave in, just like her mother did when she found out her second husband had been raping Denise from the age of ten. The pattern was set.

At least Denise could save her unborn daughter the same pain. As the baby kicked, a gunshot echoed through the house.

The phone rang. It was eight o'clock.

Tiny Little Feet

I don't think they have a stated size for her. Less than the size of a grape, her tiny heart pounds away, keeping her alive for another minute. She shouldn't be here yet, she's not ready. Blue veins, fragile but strong, pump blood through to the vital organs, struggle hard for her to survive.

A week ago I could have had her legally terminated. Today, a delicate flower, attached to machines instead of to me, she lies in a soft incubator, breathing with the aid of pumped oxygen.

Her little pink hat warms her head, smaller than a tennis ball with tiny eyes tight shut.

A little mouth opens to a gap as her body involuntary yawns. My eyes tingle with hot tears and love. I watch her sleep.

The nurse said I could touch her but I dare not. I'm frightened she might break, disintegrate in my fingers like the dust she could have been last week. Would have been had I not changed my mind.

And I'm so glad I did.

But then, in an epiphany, she was born anyway, so premature they didn't expect her to survive. It's a miracle she has. Hope surges through me, filling me with confidence. My darling daughter has given me this, and I reach out and touch her.

And count.

Two tiny little feet and ten tiny little toes.

The Birch Family
Steve

Death of an Antichrist

So, you stand before me, your God. Called here in an instant, not even dead. These are special circumstances. You must answer to me now and truthfully.

I was just being aware of a sparrow's fall when I heard you talking about the death of your Antichrist. Why do you support such a being? How was he yours? How did he die?

Yes, you might well cower. I created all. I gave you my son to die for your sins. I called him Christ and he gave his all that you might have some hope. Thus you repay me.

Tell me now, young man, and fear my retribution. I am as old as time itself and have power beyond imagination.

Oh, sorry. The death of your Aunty Chris. I do apologise.

I did say I was old, you know.

Under Canvas

Prompt: as title

It had been raining for two days and it was all I could do not to cry. Eleven years old, I was away for two weeks, camping with my 'friends' in the scouts. The first time away from my parents for more than a day or two at a time, I missed them acutely and the rain had been pocking on the canvas forever.

Precocious, but lacking substance, I suffered. I didn't have the strength, the backbone, to see me through. We played a game of hide and seek the day before in a welcome, but treacherous, hour of dryness and the patrol leader made me hold his dick as a forfeit because I was found first. Daft things like this happened in the cubs, but this was different. We used to giggle, but he didn't laugh at all, he just breathed funny and it was big like my dad's, not like mine or my friends'.

'You can share my two-man tent tonight, no need to be crowded like that. I love it under canvas!'

A voice strained with jollity still makes me sweat.

Elizabeth (aged 11 years)

Box of Monkeys

I work at the zoo. I overheard we were getting something, but had no idea what.

Finally, the big van arrived. I ripped open the large boxes.

They were full of . . .

Suspense . . .

I bet you think I'm going to say 'monkeys', don't you?

Well . . .

Drum roll . . .

No! It was . . . bamboo for the pandas!

There was a great big box of monkeys waiting for that package!

The Toy Box

I am determined to get rid of those old toys.

Right, let's get cracking. How do you work this eBay thing? Right, list an item . . . ok, let's get the kids' old toy box – the worn-out Jack in the Box. Yep, this has to go. The kids haven't looked at it in years!

No – this is what Amy was playing with when she said her first words – 'Jacky box'. I can't get rid of this!

I know, the building blocks. Oh no – Sandy coloured them in all her favourite colours and named each of them. She called them her children. How could I think of getting rid of those!

Ah, Izzie's Baby Benjamin. Wait – this was her first birthday present! I could never sell that!

Oh dear, this isn't working. Let's try something else – I know! Not eBay – Amazon!

Matthew (aged 9 years)

The Wandering Soul

Prompt: Tombstoning

If hell is bad, school is worse, and home can be even worse, then I must be having a really bad day because home seems even worse than usual. That's effectively summing up my life, Ricky thinks while munching on his Hershey Bar. My friends aren't even my friends any more, in fact they weren't even my friends in the first place, if I had just agreed to stay in the hidden realm and stay a spirit, but no I have to be solid.

Humans don't even have decent names! I mean, come on: Ricky, Gaylord, Herman, what is it with this planet and solid people made of mostly water. Mostly water, yet they are solid. Whassup wit da way they speak, like? I'm goin' insane man. Okay now I'm gonna try to write normally for whoever's reading it, mainly because I want you to find out the secret of my treasure . . .

Firstly, I shall tell you the story of how I got my treasure. There were a lot of thieves back in 1,620 BC, when I was twelve. I crossed at that age, though I'm seventeen now.

My crossing story is very interesting so you have got to hear it, or at least read it. My story starts in Mexico and finishes in Texas, hung from a tree. I hung there for three days and nights before I was completely mutilated. I was still dead four weeks later, by then my death advisor had sewn me back together and left me without a scratch. I came back as a spirit, but I then I chose to return as a human. That's my story. I found some liquidised gold and I spent another 2,000-odd years finding out how to solidify the gold.

I found out how just in 2578. It would take at least twenty-two years, not including how long it will take to get the equipment. I need Trongmekwings and Shmingloogles. I can get them from Purlingwon 4, (the 83rd planet from the sun). Getting there won't be hard, it will just be getting the equipment.

Now I'm on Purlingwon 4 and I've acquired the Trongmekwings, there are a few problems with getting the Shmingloogles. There are a few too many aliens trying to stop me getting away with them, I've just got the last one.

I have just got away from Purlingwon 4, but I've run out of fuel on Catacrom 4. I know a source of fuel but it's very hard to acquire and there are no shops that sell it. There is only one other source of fuel – human hair – which I have a lot of. For the first time in my life, I'm having a haircut.

Yes, I feel significantly lighter since I had that haircut. Before, I weighed ten and a half stone, now I weigh eight and a half. I have made the gold and I am looking for a place other than Galactonoso to bury and hide it. But since there seems to be nowhere else I'll just have to go there.

There it's buried so the lucky reader of this has now got the chance to get treasure.

Lauren Rogers

When There's Nowhere Else To Go

She looked around and started off down the street, clutching the shopping bags. When she approached a group of youths standing outside the Post Office she crossed the road, glancing behind to make sure they weren't following. The bags became heavier and heavier as she struggled on, so she stopped and put them down for a moment. She rubbed the red marks on her hands, picked the bags up in a different order and went on her way. Not much further to go now. She walked past the big houses on Maple Street, the windows glowing with Christmas lights, doors bedecked with wreaths. Past the adverts for flashy new mobile phones and the latest fizzy pop creation. Past the estate agent with its brightly lit windows. She stopped and looked at 'her' house. Red brick, sash windows, door in the middle. Still not sold.

She reached the end of the road where the cars streaked by on the motorway flyover. Underneath the grey concrete structure were several saggy cardboard boxes, an old brazier and piles of rubbish. A group of people in large grey coats were huddled around the small fire, passing around a bottle.

'Hey, Rebecca,' old George called out to her. 'We've got mince pies here! Come an' get one!'

The Toy Box

Staring at the screen, May-Lee clicked randomly on the pictures. She was tired and wanted to go to bed, but it wasn't time yet. Mother said she had another ten minutes to play. But she didn't want to play. She was bored and she was tired. She wished that she could read, but Mother said it wasn't time to learn to read yet. Not until she was eight. But she could read some words. Like her name and some of the little words. But she hadn't told Mother. She daren't tell Mother.

She leant back in her chair and rubbed her eyes with the backs of her hands. She glanced at her bed and the blue curtains. There was nothing else to look at in the room. She turned back to the screen. Ah. Here was Mother.

'Tidy away the toy box now, May-Lee. Bedtime in two minutes.'

May-Lee clicked at the toys and put them back in the box. She saved her favourite giraffe until last. She loved the way his neck was all floppy. She wished she could actually touch him.

'That's it. Good girl. Now into bed.' Mother disappeared from the screen and May-Lee slipped from her chair and into bed, pulling up the blue cover around her and hugging herself tightly.

Once

Prompt: Once in a lifetime, never in mine

It only happened once. Strange, isn't it? What things can you think of that only happen once? Your first day at school. Your first kiss (and the rest). Getting married (maybe?). Being born. Your first word. Can you think of anything else? Your first step. The first time you got a wage packet. Have a think and see what you come up with.

Well there's one other first that you probably won't remember. But I do. It was the turning point in my life. It was the first time I saw pink. All my life there had been black.

Just black.

All day.

Every day.

Noises around me and having no idea what the noises looked like. People, family, friends, and not knowing what they looked like. Walking and not knowing where to. Reading about the world through my fingertips and not able to visualise a boat, a plane, a flower, a snowstorm. Just that blackness. And a few flashes of brightness now and again.

Then the accident. Getting hit by a bus and cracking my head on the pavement. And then opening my eyes to your face. Your beautiful pink face.

Gary Hewitt

Inspiration

Prompt: Once in a lifetime, never in mine

What to write, what to do? He was an author, a man who could command worlds at his fingertips. Now though, pacing to and fro, his one thought was:

'I can't write!'

He thought about a story where the world was invaded, another where the ocean eats the land, another where history becomes the future. Each time he started, he could not escape beyond the first sentence.

'These ideas are crap! They are plain silly.'

In a huff, he dragged out a pair of comfortable boots. He grabbed a beige jacket, took out his phone and hurled it at the settee. A tartan scarf decorated his neck and he rushed outside to embrace the Libran air.

It helped to walk. It made his thoughts become lucid, made him feel good. It wasn't long before he left the village of Meresham, saw a stile and sped towards a familiar footpath. The sun surprised him with its warmth and he cursed being overdressed.

However, he knew how fickle the weather could be so he endured.

It wasn't long before he had the dubious pleasure of company. A haggard shrew, adorned in fake fur and stick of birch approached. The writer's face twitched when her dog saw a new plaything.

'I'm sorry, he's going to jump up at you.'

'Well, do something about it you stupid woman,' he muttered.

The collie barked in delirium when he came within striking distance and all the while his owner barked:

'Spider, come here. Spider! Spider!'

The dog bounded into Darren Carter's chest, smearing muddy paws across a suede coat. The author smiled and sought to appease the mutt with his palm.

'Bad dog Spider. Bad dog,' admonished his owner.

Darren was rewarded with another splattering of wet earth before his owner at last took hold of Spider's collar.

'Sorry. He always does that.'

Darren wondered if there was some bizarre trophy room in the dog's kennel filled with images of muddied human jackets.

'It doesn't matter, these things happen,' he lied.

Soon he was free of cur and female. With relief he found a stile. The woods awaited and if there was a story to be found he'd find it here all right. Always, the gentle breeze in the leaves offered a sonorous whisper to his creative whims. He ambled for a solid ten minutes before he spotted something incongruous. A leaf strewn path veered deep into the trees. Bewitched, he decided to investigate. He wondered how long the new path had been there when he discerned a slight sniffle.

He pulled up sharp, but all he could see where the ubiquitous thorns of a blackberry bush. He listened, concerned, but there was nothing. With a shrug, he stepped forward once more when a faint female voice pleaded with him.

'Please help.'

'Hello. Is anyone there?'

The sound came from behind the blackberry bushes once again, but their formidable defence daunted Darren's adventurous endeavours.

'Miss? I can't see you. Can you tell me where you are?'

'I'm right here. Right underneath the thorns.'

Darren stooped. What he saw took his breath away. Beneath the bramble's tentacles was a circle of red toadstools. At their centre stood a wonderful tiny lady dressed in purple and white with waspish wings.

'What . . . What, who are you?'

'I'm Melanie Sloe. A fairy Queen but I've been hurt. Can you help?'

Darren glanced around, eager not to be discovered.

'Of course, what can I do?'

Melanie reached out her hand and touched the tip of Darren's outstretched finger. He found himself enveloped in a shroud of joy.

'Take me to your home. I don't think I'll last out here in the wild like this.'

Darren opened his palm and invited the fey sprite to clamber on. She accepted and with great care he took possession of her delicate body.

'Thank you so much. Is it far to your home?'

'Not far at all. Look, I'm going to have to put you into my pocket. It's safer in there but it'll be dark.'

'That's okay, Darren. I can make my own light, thank you.'

The author wondered how she had discerned his name when Melanie reminded him she was a fairy. Knowing his name was simple magic.

Darren began his journey home. He was grateful for this once in a lifetime opportunity and even more grateful at the wonderful story he'd just inherited.

Machine Spirit
Prompt: Natural Selection

Death was waiting.

'Get him in here.'

Ninety four years and he could feel life weakening. His brain was sharp though, these last ten years he'd been preparing for this moment.

'Hook Mr Power's temple to the transferral unit. Now for God's sake! Yes, blue wire, slap on plenty of gel. Come on people, get busy.'

George Power managed to glimpse a young mouse of a girl stick a hypodermic in. The pain should have been instant. Instead, he felt a slight numbing of his left side.

'Damn, his pulse is dangerously low. If we don't shape up we'll lose him.'

The medics began to blur. George's eyes felt so heavy under the belligerent attack of time. He daren't let them shut.

'We ready for transferral yet? Sharon?'

'All set, Dr Littlewoods. Shall I engage?'

The eyes yielded and death stepped forward. His bitter fingers grabbed the gentle sinews of George Power's heart and squeezed. It wouldn't be long.

'Go, go, go.'

A violent hum screamed into the dying patient's brain. He felt himself rising, entering a flashing in a treacle hue. He glanced back to his body lapsing to the joy of demise.

'Got him. We've got him Dr Littlewoods.'

The doctor swept the last beads of sweat beneath his greying brow. It'd been too close.

'Okay everyone, time to find out if it worked.'

A nervous finger struck the execute key. An interminable

silence ensued.

'What's happening? We should have him by now?'

'It's okay Doctor. It can take a while for the search programme to work.'

The monitor at Dr Littlewoods's desk brightened. First, a few distant dots began to form a silhouette. Seconds passed and the image of a young powerful man took residence and etched upon the avatar's face was the smirk of success.

'Mr Power, you okay Sir?'

The spirit in the machine's panellised eyes blinked. All those millions he spent, all those man hours in anticipation for this one selfish moment.

'Sir?'

'Never better Jim. My thanks to you all and by God I didn't think death would feel so damn great.'

George didn't care when his wizened broken body was removed and taken to the incinerators.

'Who needed flesh and blood anyway.'

Simple Solution

Prompt: Simple Minds, Simple Times

The Minister looked again and again. The hard facts told him drug-related offences had risen over nine per cent in the last year alone. He was damned if he was going to carry the can. A nervous tap on the door snapped away his precious attention.

'Enter.'

A ferret of a man made his way into his master's chamber. He sat at the indicated position.

'Damn piss poor figures, Alistair. Nine percent rise this year. One bloody year, can you believe it?'

'I know Mr. Utherscott. It's pretty poor.'

The Home Secretary continued to shake his head before planting his skull atop his raised hands.

'Bloody press calling for me head; say we're doing nothing at all whilst skagheads run the country.'

Alistair shook his head obsequiously. It had served him well, years of servitude.

'Trouble is Al, what are we going to bloody well do? If I send the police in, I'll
have those human rights twats on me back. If I try softly, softly, the press'll say it's the victims who suffer. I can't bloody win.'

'Maybe we should give the criminals what they want Sir.'

Joe Utherscott blinked incredulously at his underling.

'What are you on about? You telling me I should give them drugs?'

Alistair Birch nodded.

'Indeed. Sir, I've heard of a drug which can snare the user after one small dose. They become addicted instantly and they are unable to function unless they find another tablet in twenty four hours.'

His employer bristled with indifference.

'And.'

'Well, there is a side effect.'

'Go on, get on with it.'

'Fatality.'

Ten years ago Joe Utherscott would have sacked Alistair Cowling on the spot. Now, with pressure unbearable, the drastic action deserved thought.

'You're saying extermination?'

'I wouldn't call it extermination Sir, merely the users getting the ultimate high. The bottom line is that those who don't use drugs would be perfectly fine.'

'Whilst the abusers cease to become a problem . . . Trouble is, it sounds a bit too like Heinrich Himmler, still a bit of tough could be just what this country needs.' The Home Secretary clapped.

'I like it Al, I bloody like it. One thing though, if we go ahead with this no-one can ever trace it to us. We'd be lynched.'

'It's all very hush hush, Sir. Only a few people are aware at such an embryonic stage. Once we get it out on the streets, primary research indicates a term of six months before drug dependency ceases to become a problem.'

'A simple solution to a complicated problem. Bloody good job.'

Waterfall

Prompt: Pump Action

The soldier could feel his speeding heart.

'Sergeant Briggs. I'm at the break point.'

His voice seemed alien amid the silence of the Arndale Centre. With condition quarantine and enemy unknown, Private Grigson was eager for his colleagues to catch up.

'Soldier, hold position and look for anything strange. Me and Zebra team en route. Get your safety off just in case.'

Grigson found no amusement at the Sergeant's jest. Instead, he brandished his weapon and scanned the array of shops where the hidden could lurk. Grigson continued to search. His attention wavered on a burger bar when he thought he saw movement. He hated the tricks his imagination could play. It was improbable for the enemy to be so close so early. Again. No mistake. A flutter of green and black bobbed up before ducking to the haven of an empty counter.

'Sarge, positive sighting of hostile. Repeat, positive sighting of hostile.'

'Continue to hold. E.T.A to you two minutes. Only engage if hostile attacks.'

The walkie-talkie's echo snapped the disturbed interloper to attention. The enemy boasted its height of over eight feet. It tired of the coarse fare from the rancid kitchen and examined the insignificant repast staring back.

It moved fast. In a xenomorphic heartbeat the beast was half way across the aisle, claws unsheathed, fangs exposed. It saluted Private Grigson with a terrible war cry. John Grigson fired his first round and the salvo passed harmlessly into a row of Happy Birthday Nan cards on a stall to the creature's left. It would be on him within a second. John found the speed to shoot again.

The shell caught the alien in the centre of the forehead. A vortex of flailing limbs crashed. Grigson fired again, again, again until he was sure the target was liquidated. His gun was empty. A strong hand grabbed his shoulder.

'You okay son? Sorry we couldn't get here sooner.'

John shrugged and pointed.

'Impressive shooting, Private. Shame there's not much left for the boys in research. Who'd believe a water pistol could do so much damage.'

John said a private prayer of thanks to the scientists. They found the creature's critical weakness. Good old fashioned H_20.

Stef Hall

Devil Dance

Prompt: Quicksand

When you dance with the devil, you're dancing on quicksand. His shoes are shiny, not scuffed by the sands of time, and he glides effortlessly, never sinking. That, of course, is his trick: to make you want to be like him, to make you ready to give anything to dance like that, to move the way that he does.

For while he turns and quicksteps with ease, you struggle and fight to stay in time and not only must you know the steps but you must follow him so exactly and so quickly that the sand does not have time to register the difference. Put a foot wrong and you can lose a shoe. Twice, and you lose your foot.

That's how he tricks you, because he's one hell of a dancer, the devil. He cuts a dashing figure in his sharp red suit as he leads you in the Tango of Temptation, your dress singes when he whirls you too close to the edges of the dance floor and your hair comes loose through numerous lifts and daring dips. You cling to his arms for dear redemption, but sweat makes you slippery against his marble-cold red skin and the harder you hold on the more his skin slips through your grasp, until you fall into the sand are swallowed whole and delivered to hell.

We all dance with the devil every day, trying to avoid the quicksand of cigarettes, alcohol, chocolate and myriad different temptations we've thrown in our own paths. The broken promises of, 'I'll do it tomorrow' and, 'I'll start the diet *next* week', make whirlpools and eddies that suck greedily at our feet as we try to steer the devil's dance around them. And we blame him, we curse his very name.

It's not his fault, of course, it never has been. We tempt ourselves and our wills are weak, but the devil dances because he is lonely. He misses the heavenly host, he misses companionship for he sees us only briefly, for the duration of the dance until we fall. Yet he keeps dancing, he keeps searching for the perfect partner, the one who can mirror his every step and not be lost to the quicksand beneath. He believes that if he can find perfect harmony with another, can move in sure grace and perfection in time with one of God's favourite creations, that his benevolent maker will show him mercy.

And so, the devil dances.

Jobsworth

Prompt: Ragged staircarpet

The house depressed her. Everything was scrupulously clean and the woman that now sat opposite her had red, chapped hands that moved restlessly while they talked, turning against one another in a manner that spoke to Miss Pritchard of anxiety, and an aversion to being still.

The woman had been vacuuming when Miss Pritchard arrived, hair the colour of dirty straw yanked back into a ponytail and wearing an apron with a big pocket on the front that held a grubby duster and a can of Mr Muscle, even though it was only eight forty-five in the morning. The ragged stair carpet that she'd been going over, with an ancient Hoover upright that wheezed and spluttered and was probably older than Miss Pritchard, was threadbare in places, showing the floorboards, but spotlessly clean.

'When you got three kids, takes a lot of keeping up with,'

the woman explained apologetically as she turned off the vacuum cleaner and showed Miss Pritchard into the small, shabby sitting room.

The woman offered tea, which Miss Pritchard accepted, and which came in a chipped Simpsons mug. She always accepted the offer of tea or coffee; she thought it made her look as though she thought herself to be just like them, in spite of her suits and posh accent.

Now the woman sat nervously opposite Miss Pritchard and the Benefits Inspector decided that this was one of the times she really hated her job. This woman did the best she could for her family, it wasn't fair that the rules called her a cheat.

'Do you know why I'm here, Mrs Logan?' Miss Pritchard asked.

Mrs Logan ducked her head. 'You've come about me benefits, Miss.'

Miss Pritchard gritted her teeth and pressed on. 'Someone has reported that you've been doing some work on the side, Mrs Logan, and not declaring it.'

Terror washed across the woman's face. 'It's only a bit of mending sometimes, for them fellas as has no woman to do for 'em! They only give me a couple of quid.'

'Nevertheless,' Miss Pritchard said. 'Did you realise that if you don't declare all your income to the Job Centre, you're committing fraud?'

The woman started to cry.

An hour later, Miss Pritchard knocked on the door of her supervisor's office. The shoulder of her suit was still damp from where Mrs Logan had poured out her family woes: including a leaking toilet, a broken washing machine that meant she had to wash everything by hand because she couldn't afford the launderette, and now 'our Sam' had to go to the hospital for tests because his wee had gone a funny colour.

'I'm handing in my notice,' Miss Pritchard said, and threw her report on the Logans onto her supervisor's desk. 'I've decided doing this job's more than my life's worth.'

Missing

Prompt: When there's nowhere else to go

I went home. It seemed the thing to do, but there was nobody there. I sat on the doorstep because home is where you go when there's nowhere else. They're supposed to take you in, but I expect that probably works better when they know you're coming. I wondered why I hadn't gone back to the flat for my key, but it was a bit late for that. The flat was roughly seventy miles away and probably full of police by now.

It was getting dark and chilly. I suspected that once they realised I'd fled London, the parents' place was probably the first place they'd look for me, but I was here now and didn't really have any idea of what to do next. I'd kind of been counting on Dad to help me with his sly way of thinking. He'd know what to do.

But for all I knew he and Mum were sunning themselves on a tropical beach somewhere while I froze on their doorstep.

The girl seemed to come from nowhere, as though a section of jumbled moonlight and shadow suddenly took form. She walked across the gravel towards me, but it didn't crunch and when I leaned down and looked along, I could see moonlight the other side of her feet where she hovered a couple of inches off the ground.

She wore a three-quarter length army greatcoat, hands in

the pockets, which she drew closer around herself as she sat next to me on thin air.

'You took some finding,' she said.

I looked down. 'I'm not ready.'

'I don't mean to be harsh: but tough.'

I let out a humourless laugh. 'They're supposed to take you in when you go home. I wasn't expecting them not to be here. I thought I could stay.'

A shadow crossed the girl's face and her voice sounded hollow. 'No one gets to stay.'

'So that's it? That's all I get?'

The girl stood and turned away from me. 'You get the same as everyone else,' she held out a hand. 'You get a lifetime.'

I sighed and put my hand in hers. 'Okay. Will they miss me?'

She looked back and the ghost of a smile touched her lips.

'Yes, they'll miss you.'

Running From and To

Prompt: Open road

The open road was in some ways worse than a blank page and she sat there, staring at it in anxiety. After a while, she switched off the engine; the only sounds the relentless drumming of the rain, the swish-flap of the windscreen wipers and the tick of cooling metal. The windows of the Ford Fiesta started to fog.

Cars swept past. Some drivers beeped horns; others gave her looks of disdain as she sat on the grass verge before the slip-road down to the M1. No one seemed in the slightest bit concerned; they just thought she was parked illegally and bloody ignorant.

The problem was she didn't know where she was running to. Her back was starting to hurt so she prised her clammy fingers from the furry steering-wheel cover her teenage daughter insisted on – could a steering wheel get cold? – and sat back in the driver's seat, picking florescent pink fluff out of the creases between her fingers. 'From' was sorted, 'from' was easy, she could write a book about 'from' . . . well, no, perhaps she couldn't, and that was the thing, wasn't it? Nevertheless, 'from' was a done deal.

But 'to' was a big mystery and that was what stopped her pulling onto the motorway. She couldn't just drive around aimlessly with no plan in mind: sooner or later she would run out of petrol, food, or worse, fear and then she'd be stuck in the middle of nowhere and have to call the AA out again. They were so used to her now they just rolled their eyes and towed her home.

She thought about the computer, sitting at home with its terrifying white screen and that greedily blinking cursor sitting in the top corner, waiting to be fed. The idea of going back and sitting down before it again twisted her stomach. Then she recalled the resigned look on the face of the AA man, the 'Oh God, not this nutter again' look and redness crept from the collar of her shirt.

She reached out, flicked on the heating and watched the fog on the windows start to shrink and evaporate, while fear and embarrassment battled for supremacy in her stomach.

Five minutes later, she turned the ignition and drove.

When Jeff got home, Megan was at the computer. The two already-published books of her trilogy lay open at two of the myriad bookmarks strewn throughout them and, as she worked, Megan glanced spasmodically at the calendar where the publisher's deadline was marked with a big red 'X', circled five times.

He dropped a kiss on the top of her head. 'Been for a drive again, have we?'

'I only went as far as the slip-road today,' she said, not looking up.

As he went through to the kitchen to make dinner, Jeff recalled briefly the day

they found his missing wife in New Zealand and brought her back under sedation. According to the New Zealand police, she had been screaming about the blank page when they found her.

He supposed the slip-road was progress.

Seeing the Funny Side

Prompt: CCTV

Gladys regarded her teenage son's pimply, naked arse and sniffed.

'When you told me you were gonna be on the telly, I didn't think CCTV was what you had in mind,' she said.

'Mum, will you turn around!' Jason was red in the face as he struggled into the spare clothes she had brought for him.

Gladys snorted. 'So you'll parade around the centre of town as naked as the day you were born, but you don't want me to see your bare arse? I used to wipe that arse, my boy.'

Jason cringed and finally managed to get both legs into the right holes of his boxer shorts and pull them up. 'We don't have to go into all that again, do we Mum?'

Gladys held his jeans out to him and watched as he staggered around the room, trying to get them on. 'If you stopped taking your kit off every time you'd had a few, we wouldn't need to go into it at all.'

'Yes Mum,' Jason resorted to sitting on the bed and squirming around until he had his jeans on. He seemed to have left his equilibrium behind, probably wherever he'd left the clothes he'd gone out in that night.

Once Jason was dressed, they emerged from the cell to the smirks of the local coppers. This was a weekly occurrence and one which some of the more jaded cops had started to look forward to. The stoic expression on Gladys' face when she plodded down to the station with Jason's spare clothes every Friday night was almost worth the paperwork the arrest generated.

The release papers signed, the desk sergeant gave them the weekly talking to. They both sat in stoic silence, nodding in all the right places. It was almost like a script.

'Look Jason,' he said when he was done with the formal stuff. 'This is going to have to stop. You'll be eighteen in three weeks, and then we won't be able to let you off so lightly, do you understand?'

'Oh he understands, Sergeant, and he won't do it again, will you Jason?' Gladys supplied.

'No, Mum,' Jason said dutifully.

The sergeant leaned across the desk and winked. 'Tho' between you and me son,' he said. 'I'm going to miss your bare-arsed cheek!'

Stoned to Death
Prompt: Stone in my shoe

Being married to you was like a stone in my shoe. At first I didn't really notice it; the stone was stuck right in the tip of the shoe and was little more than a pressure against my big toe. A slight imposition on my style, a minor infringement on my space, not much different.

After a bit of a walk, the stone started stabbing me in the bottom of the foot at every step. Your sullen silences when I won the battle of the remote control, the petulant tantrums when I did something without consulting you. Your testosterone spread out and got comfy; a married man, king of the castle, the lord and master and all those other things that men expect women to do to congratulate them on being masters of the Universe. Anything I did that you didn't like was met with jabs and bruises; didn't I think I maybe ought to go on a diet? Didn't I think I was a bit too old for that outfit?

Like wearing boots with so many laces it would be impractical to stop and remove the stone, our marriage was something I had committed myself to and society dictated that I grin and bear it. I got used to the stone, grew callouses and learned to accommodate it, limping and scurrying from place to place, trying to do the things I wanted when you wouldn't notice; it was easier to adapt my life than to have that argument again. If I kept my head down and my gob shut and made sure your dinner was on the table at six sharp and the girls already bathed and in bed, you didn't notice me, and that was good.

When you had a heart attack, my first response was not wifely concern, but an unfurling in the pit of my stomach it took me ages to work out was relief. I rushed to the hospital as expected, one sleepy pyjama'd child under each arm, when the call came. I sat by your bedside, face pinched in what they took to be concern whilst in my head I concentrated on unlacing that boot. It wasn't easy, the laces were stiff from neglect and old age, a lifetime of broken dreams and shattered self-esteem lay over them like cobwebs, but inch by inch they started to give.

You never woke, and when they told me there was nothing they could do, I wept tears of release while the relief in my stomach unfurled into a flag of me.

At the cemetery, as I stepped forward and threw the handful of dirt down onto your coffin, I shook the stone from my shoe.

I'd forgotten how comfortable shoes can be without a stone in them. I can walk straight without compensating for those jabs in the sole of my foot, and I hold my head high and walk at my own pace.

I think it's time for a new pair.

The Cusp

Prompt: Magic bullets

When she tried to pinpoint the exact moment it happened, Kinkaid kept coming back to the lecture he'd given her on magic bullets. It had really been a gradual thing, of course, but even with gradual things she was convinced there was a cusp, a single defining moment, when the flip happens and what had been started being something else.

If she could find it, she could pin it down like a butterfly on a board and analyse the hell out of it. She was pretty sure it wasn't meant to happen, it hadn't been in anyone's game plan. In fact, she wasn't convinced it wasn't actually forbidden. Either way, she needed to get it dealt with before it got her killed one way or another.

Sorensen wasn't human. She wasn't sure exactly what he was and hadn't yet plucked up the courage to ask, but no human had eyes like pools of liquid mercury; silvery and restless they shifted and changed like steam rolling across the surface of a fathomless lake. Staircases and corridors leading into complexity so great she could only grasp one corner of it.

Sometimes when he touched her without his gloves, she saw things in his eyes she didn't know if she was supposed to see. When his skin touched hers, cool like a sea breeze, she saw reflections in his eyes of things the way he saw them. The world in his eyes was a strange and alien place but beautiful, as though he saw things, saw people, as they really were without any of the physical crap getting in the way.

Under his supervision, she had focused her will into a crystalline representation of what she thought a bullet looked like. It was as long as the first knuckle of her thumb and colours writhed within it as she filled it with her energy.

'The beauty of these things,' Sorry said as he watched her pouring her intent into the magic bullet,' is that they're as deadly as the real thing, but they leave no physical evidence.'

She raised her hand, squinting as she readied the bullet for flight towards the tin cans Sorensen had set up on the garden wall. 'I thought we weren't supposed to use magic to kill.'

He sighed. 'Normally, no, but you are special, Kinkaid, you will need to defend yourself.'

She jerked towards him, eyes frightened, and lost control

over the bullet. She felt it swivel in her palm, turning back upon herself and his hand lashed out, snake-like, and covered her own, cancelling her magic with his.

'Concentrate!' he chided.

And in his eyes she saw herself. The same long red hair, the same green eyes and small, spare frame. As ordinary as she ever had been and yet she burned in his eyes, she blazed in glory and in strength, a beauty far beyond what any human man would see.

And that was it. The cusp, the moment.

That was when Kinkaid fell in love with him.

The Way Things Are Done

Prompt: Grandpa's chair

My grandparents' house was the hub of the family; an exciting place, full of relatives who came and went like buses, some of them bringing tribes of cousins for me to play with, some of them who gave me a shiny 50p and sent me down to the sweetie shop.

The whole house was chaos and noise. My Nana got no rest: fetching and carrying, preparing meals and snacks and making coffee from the time she got up until she lay her weary bones to rest long after midnight. When I was older, I helped her with the chores and the fetching and carrying because my bones were younger than hers, and who kept grandchildren and barked themselves?

Things were always moving, people and furniture, in an intricate daily dance to which only my family knew the steps. Visitors watched us all with bemusement, not quite sure how we all knew which way to go.

The only thing that didn't move was Grandpa. He sat in his armchair, bang in front of the telly, only moving to go to the loo. Everything else came to him, and even when we were kids no one dared get in his seat while he was gone.

He sat there like some benign old statue, head of the household. He was a good man and a kindly one, but old and set in his old-fashioned ways. He expected things to be done in a certain fashion, and that was how they were done. No one had to teach me how to measure out just the right amount of sugar for his tea, or how to stir it just the right number of times, that was just the way it had always been done.

When he died, his chair sat empty. He'd been gone a long time, yet still no one dared to sit there. I didn't understand; it was just a chair, why didn't anyone sit in it? I asked my mother, and she said it was just the way things were done.

One morning, while Nana was still in bed, I sat in Grandpa's chair. I was nervous, almost expecting to feel some sense of wrongness, but it was just a chair. I turned on the telly and enjoyed the best view in the room.

When my Nana came down and saw me sitting in Grandpa's chair, she cried. She sank into her own seat, staring at me with tears clinging to her papery skin. Guiltily I jumped out of the chair, turning off the telly.

'Nana, I'm sorry. I don't understand why no one sits in it.'

Nana patted the arm of her own chair and I perched next to her as she took my hand.

'I like to keep it empty. It reminds me that he was there, that he loved me.'

'I'm sorry, I didn't know.'

'Sometimes, Clara,' she said, 'there's a reason for the way things are done.'

The Ripples

Prompt: Ripple in time

'You've told them that, Derek,' my grandmother's voice was weary.

She had said the same thing at least seven times already that afternoon. My grandfather looked crestfallen, and I wondered why she did it. It wasn't like anyone really minded hearing the same stories over and over again, and we all knew he couldn't help it. Alzheimer's, the doctor's called it, a fairly recently discovered condition in comparison to the lives of my grandparents.

Soft in the head, my grandmother called it. She was that kind of brisk, no-nonsense woman whose response to any kind of emotional outburst was to chivvy the person along until they got over it. She hadn't seemed to grasp the idea that chivvying her husband along wasn't going to help, he wasn't going to get any better. I think she was afraid.

'It's like there's ripples in time,' he confided to me one day. 'It's all distorted. Some things I can't remember at all, though your Nanny tells me about it. Like you . . . I know who you are, but I can't for the life of me remember you being born. Other things are just . . . wrong. I think I remember, but then they tell me I've got it all back to front. I'm all in a muddle and I can't seem to keep things straight in my head any more.'

He looked frightened and I remember thinking that a great big man like him shouldn't be afraid of anything.

After that, we never called it by its proper name in our family, it was always The Ripples. Made it sound friendlier, somehow, something we could cope with a lot better than Alzheimer's.

Last week, I went to visit Mum and drop off a few things I picked up for her when I went into the city. She avoids places with a lot of people these days, she says it confuses her. She even goes to Tesco really early in the morning to do her shopping.

I nipped to the loo while I was there, and I noticed that she'd taken the towels for washing, and hadn't remembered to put new ones out. I thought I'd do her a favour and when I opened the airing cupboard door I found a bag of frozen carrots sitting among the neatly folded towels.

I went through to the living room, holding the dripping article between my thumb and forefinger.

'What the heck was this doing in the airing cupboard, Mum?'

She looked surprised, then shook her head. 'The Ripples must be catching up to me at last!'

She laughed, but she sounded frightened.

Claire Nixon

Grandpa's Chair

In Grandpa's chair
he'd tell us a tale
of those who died
in that long last day
he'd silently weep
as he tells his tale
so full of pride
together we pray
of those that sleep

In Grandpa's chair
I sit telling his tale
of those who died
in that long last day
I silently weep
as I tell his tale
so full of pride
together we pray
of those that sleep
alongside Grandpa

Loving the Enemy

We exchanged hellos and photographs
But we never did say goodbye
We never had the chance to say I love you
Or to share our anguish and despair
Or to cry upon each other's shoulder
About our loved ones waiting back at home

We exchanged food for drink
But we never did say goodbye
We never had the chance to become close
Yet we tended each other's wounds
Yet we shared our fears on Christmas Day
About our concerns of how it will end

We exchanged hellos and photographs
But we never did say goodbye
I wish I could have been with you
So you knew that someone cared
So you knew that someone loved you
And now it is time for my last breath too – alone

Natural Selection

On all fours Carrie scrubbed the kitchen tiles with a wire brush, her hands gleamed red, white knuckles protruded. Tears streamed down her swollen face washing away the goo from her nose. She was too afraid to wipe her nose, too afraid to wipe the tears away, too afraid to tell him where to go.

'Hurry the fuck up, woman. I want my dinner.' He sat on the wooden chair with his legs spread wide, in between them the oversized Doberman panted, saliva hanging in large droops. 'Who's a good boy? Eh? Come on. Who's a good boy? Yes he is.' He patted the dog's head and ruffled its flab around the neck. 'I know . . . it was all her fault. Not letting you outside to do your business, fucking bitch ain't she? Yes she is. Who wants a doggie treat?'

Carrie kept her head lowered. It wasn't her fault the dog had soiled in the kitchen. As always, he made sure she was busy when the dog was due to go out and then give it chocolate, which he knows too well gives the dog the runs.

'Once you've cleaned that shit up you can get your fat arse upstairs and clean the bathroom, I had a shave this morning and there's hairs all over the place. You know I hate it when there are hairs all over the place. It's fucking unhygienic. Some wife you are.'

He stormed past her and kicked the bucket of detergent over. 'For fuck's sake, do you have to be so clumsy! Christ, the dog has more sense than you.' He turns to the dog and pats him. 'Ain't you? Yes you have. And you're smarter than her too, ain't you . . . yes you are. Who's a good boy?'

Under her breath Carrie whispers, 'I hate you . . . I'll make you pay.'

The following week was hard for Carrie, he was laid up in

bed – ill.

'I'm dying, Carrie.'

'It's just the flu.'

'Don't be so fucking stupid, woman. It ain't the flu, it's pneumonia.'

'Here take this, it'll make you feel better.' She poured the green gloop onto the spoon.

'What the fuck is that?'

'Medicine. I bought it from the chemist this morning. It should have you on your feet within a day or so. I do miss having you around when I'm doing the housework.' She gritted her teeth and smiled.

Reluctantly he swallowed the medicine. 'Where's Max? I haven't seen him all day.'

'The dog is in the garden playing.'

'I . . . I want to see him . . . I . . . ' his words trailed off as he fell into a deep sleep.

Carrie entered the room with a tray containing a cup of coffee and a plate with several different cuts of meat on it.

'Hey, sleepy head. Wake up.' She shook him vigorously.

'Eh, yeah, when, what?' His head rolled from side to side as he tried to open his eyes.

'I don't feel too good.'

'That's because you'll be starving. Sit up, I've cooked you a meal. It has plenty of protein and iron to give you strength.'

He obeyed. 'I am a little hungry. Hmm, that does smell nice.' He picked up a fork and rammed it into a piece of meat, then shoved it in his mouth. 'Hmm, oh yes, now that is a good piece of meat.' He stuffed another in his mouth. 'What is it?'

'Just a range of natural selection cuts I prepared.' She smiled and watched him eagerly. 'Eat.'

'Carrie, where's Max?'

'Don't worry about him. He's fine.'

He peered down to his plate. 'What the fuck am I eating? I swear, if you've done anything to Max I'll fucking kill you.'

'What on earth are you talking about? Your fever is getting worse. Max is downstairs.' She opened the bedroom door and called for the dog. A few moments later the dog ran barking into the bedroom.

'Hey Max! Shit man, Carrie, I'm sorry. I dunno what I was thinking.'

'I'll send the dog back out so you can finish your meal in peace.'

She ushered the dog out of the room, sat at the bottom of the bed and watched every mouthful he took. The last piece of meat he rolled around the plate to soak up the juices then he sucked on it before he devoured it.

'I enjoyed that. Is there any left?'

'Oh there's plenty, depends what cut you want.' She pulled the blanket back. 'You've just had a bit of thigh and calf. How about a sausage and meatball sarnie later? I see that medication has worked well to numb you below the waist.'

Open Road

Tree branches swooped over the dirt track. Evan barely touched the accelerator as he tried his best to avoid the pot holes and the low branches, but his attempts were in vain. Beside him his fiancée slept. Her auburn hair was swept up high, ringlets framed her beautiful face and her painted lips were slightly open. How he wished he could take her then and now, but he knew if he disturbed her his life would not be worth living. She was in a mood as it was, they had argued over which road to take to their destination – the solitary cottage in the middle of nowhere. Of course, he no longer wanted to argue, followed her directions and now they were lost. And it was getting dark.

The further he went the denser the trees looked. A few miles back he could see open fields, now a wall of wood blocked his view. Overhead, the branches blocked what little sunlight was left of the day. With his headlights on he slowly continued. Tiredness crept over him, he felt himself drop off, but there was nothing he could do to stop it. The car jerked, he woke abruptly and looked around. Candice slept on. He opened the window. The cool air stung his face, thankfully it was enough to keep him awake for a little longer. Stifling a yawn he turned the radio on. All what could be heard was static so he switched it off.

Darkness was all around the car, even with headlights he could hardly see the road in front of him. The car no longer bounced around over pot holes and branches, he had finally came to a smooth surface, which must be tarmac as the tyres made no sound. He pressed his foot down further, the wind whipped through the window, thrashing against his face. He shivered, wound the window up and turned the heating on. The only sound that could be heard was the chattering of his teeth. Hot air was circulated throughout the car but he still shivered. He felt Candice's arms, she was warm to the touch, but his hands were icy.

He could no longer tell if trees were on either side of the road, as blackness stretched all around and the only thing he could see were the few feet of open road before him. He peered down to the clock on the dashboard, but it wasn't lit, neither were any of the dials and all of the needles pointed to zero. The engine had fallen silent too. He opened the window. He was definitely still travelling as the wind howled around him and the road in front appeared to be moving. Must be a battery fault somewhere, he'll fix it when he gets to his destination.

'Where am I?' Candice asked.

'Safe, what can you remember?'

She peered into the elderly man's eyes. 'Who are you?'

'I'm Frank, what can you remember?'

'I don't know . . . I was asleep, something woke me, a bump or something and then I fell asleep again. Where's David?'

She peered over Frank's shoulder and stared at the crumpled up car that was embedded into a tree. Beside it, on the roadside was a large black body bag.

He wasn't certain how long he'd been asleep, all he knew was when he woke up the car was still travelling and Candice was missing. He stood before the car in the headlights, calling her name; he dare not step into the thicket of blackness, something about that didn't feel right.

Eventually he climbed back into the car and turned it around; wherever she was it was somewhere back over. Cautiously, he followed the open road.

Seventeen Letters and One Reply

Dear Madeline, I was so pleased to receive your reply. I was starting to lose faith as I had sent you seventeen letters in total, but your one reply – oh what a joy. You have made my day – my week – my year. It is good to hear all is fine back home. Send my best wishes to all. I do apologise but I must make this one brief, I am being sent to the front line within the next hour. Hopefully, I will not be long there and I will be able to write to you soon. I shall take your reply with me to the front so can cast my eye across it when I am feeling alone. Take care with my son to be. I will wait in anticipation to hear the news of his birth. Yes I say son, as I know this will be true. It is my wish to call him Charles after my grandfather. Madeline do not weep for me. I am fit and well – you keep me strong. The question you seek an answer for, my darling, the answer is yes, please go and enjoy yourself. I am being called upon. Sorry for the briskness of this letter. I do love you, my Madeline.

'What's that on the back?' I turn the letter over and look at the handwritten scrawl, run my fingers across it. 'It says he died 7th August 1916.'

'Isn't that the same date it was written?'

'Yeah, he wrote this the day he died.'

'When did she receive it?'

'The envelope says January 21st 1917.'

'Must have been horrible waiting all that time to hear from him.'

'Yeah, I guess.'

'I wonder what her question was.'

'That is something we'll never find out, unless we find her letter.'

'But I still don't know why you had to call me Charles. You said his kid was called Edward.'

'Don't you get it? Since then the first born boy has been named Charles in respect.'

Charles shrugs. 'Whatever, mother. Anyway I found you, now it's my turn to hide.'

I carefully fold the letter and put it back into the

envelope and place it into the metal tin with the rest of the letters. 'Okay, go hide. I'll make you understand when you're a little older.'

'Cool. I thought Dad was coming home this week from the war.'

I smile and say, 'He was . . . he will, he'll be home soon.' I try to convince myself.

They say no news is good news, but I know that is not true.

The Postman's Bicycle

'Mummy, who's my daddy?'

'You what!?' Jane's eyes widened.

'Who's my daddy?'

'Your father is your daddy. What makes you ask?'

'Well, Macy says her mum says my dad is the milkman's cos you always had the milkman in the house when Dad was at work.'

Jane's face flushed. It took her a few moments to reply. 'Don't be so silly. That's silly talk.' She couldn't think of anything else to say. 'Best not to repeat that nonsense in front of your father.'

'So does that mean my new baby sister's dad is not the postman's?'

'NO! What makes you say that?' Jane quickly sat down and held her stomach.

'So why is the postman's bicycle left outside our house every Saturday when I get back from the park and dad is at work?'

Marit Meredith

Snowdrops

Prompt: Tiny little feet

It snowed as I neared my due date; great, fat flakes falling heavily to the ground, blanketing everything in sight, silencing every sound. The baby stirred inside me.

'Not yet my child. It's not yet time.' By morning we would be snowed in. 'All will be well,' I told her quietly. 'All will be well!' I told myself.

The image of snowdrops popped into my mind. They'd be up soon, forcing their
way through the snow. Born survivors. I pulled the shawl around my shoulders and stepped outside, into the cold whiteness, my hand smoothing my stomach.

'Do you feel that, my little one?' Stillness. Calm. I felt my baby move her tiny little feet and smiled.

Two days later the snow was gone. So were you, my precious one – into the stillness and the calm. And my garden was covered in snowdrops, remembering you.

Surprise!

Rebecca dragged the old typewriter out of the closet. She might be small, but she was strong and she didn't need any help from anyone. She knew how to use it, too. She had watched her daddy often enough, before he got his smart new computer. She wasn't allowed to use the computer yet. Sitting cross-legged on the floor, she started typing. She could spell most of the words, except for the long ones.

When Rebecca came home from school earlier that day, she had gone straight to her room for Teddy, her constant companion since she was a baby. She liked to cuddle Teddy, snuggled up on the sofa in front of the telly, while mummy cooked their tea. But Teddy was gone! Rebecca looked everywhere, turning her room upside down, but she couldn't find him anywhere. She was almost in tears when she noticed the back door ajar. Aha! They had been burgled! Somebody had stolen Teddy and they weren't going to get away with it. She knew just what to do.

Rebecca hit the keys hard, making sure every letter was sharp and clear:

Dear mister police man,
Our house was burgled today
and my Teddy was stolen.
Please will you find the thief
and get Teddy back?

From Rebecca age nearly 6

She addressed her letter to 'mister police man at the police station' in her best handwriting and ran to the post-box a few doors away. Mister police man would soon catch the thief, she was sure of that. She skipped back home, through the garden gate and up the path. Soon she would be re-united with Teddy. But wait! What was that? Rebecca did a double-take as mummy shouted 'Surprise!' There, on the washing line, pegged up by his ears and dripping wet, was Teddy, gently swaying in the breeze. All bright and clean.

O-oh!

The Way Home

From somewhere deep within, beyond
the known, the humdrum –
where the self still might dwell,
she looks out, yet again
on a journey
with no purpose.
Shuffling to and fro,
arms flailing at invisible spirits:
muttering, swearing –
grabbing at the hem of her skirt
she grins, oblivious of decorum –
doing all the things she'd never do –
in another life.

Visitors come less often,
then visits trickle to a stop,
the incomprehensible jabber
cause for unease.
'Who are you? I don't know you.
Go away.
Are you the doctor? Are you?
Where's my daddy?'
Her back turned, she wanders off
searching for the way home
wringing her hands,
trying to think, but thoughts
evade her.

Where is he?
He's gone, but she doesn't know.
He, who swore to care for her
as the demeaning took hold –

sleeping the innocents' sleep
beneath a stone:
'My beloved husband',
but she doesn't know
he's passed on, through the portal
she had hoped to reach
before the self that she had known
got lost – in the cobweb of disease.

The Toy Box

I tell you, those twins are bad boys. They make me do silly things and I don't like it. Anyway, we're going to move far, far away and they won't see me again, ever. So there!

I'm three and I've got a baby sister. I wanted to keep her in the toy box, but I'm not allowed. I can go out to play as long as Anita is there to look after me. Anita is seven and goes to school. She wears her mummy's high-heeled shoes and hats and puts lipstick on when she goes out to play. I'm not allowed. But sometimes I do, in Anita's house. Her mummy washes off the lipstick before I go home, in case Grandma is there. She doesn't like lipstick. Mummy hides hers.

My brother is six. He's a naughty boy, too, so Mummy won't let him look after me. He doesn't want to anyway. He's friends with the twins. They are horrible to my cat. I hide him in the toy box sometimes. I love my cat, but we can't take him with us, so Anita is going to look after him. Her daddy said she could. My cat has only got one eye.

I don't like packing my toys into cardboard boxes. I want them in the toy box, in my toy box. The lady on the top floor has bought the house and her boy is having my room.

And my toy box. But my cat is in the box. He doesn't like my cat. It makes him sneeze. Perhaps daddy will let me take my toy box after all. I won't tell him that the cat is still in the box.

Tight Red Dress

'My, you look pretty!' my mum said,
as I twirled in my too-tight red dress.
She twisted my hair
in a ribbon; pinned it close to my head,
hissed 'Smile!'
as she marched me to
the dance floor, filling me
with utter dread.

I knew every step,
every twist and turn, as
I practised all by myself –
but to dance with a boy
in a Ball Room?
My heart filled
with utter dread.

Sarah Star

Midnight at the Aquarium

Martin looked around the deserted halls. In the blue half-light, the aquarium took on an eerie air. As he wandered down the ramp to the deep-sea pool viewing arena, his feet pounded on the carpet. It was the only sound other than a faint bubbling of the oxygen tank.

'This was his first overnight watch. Mel put him down for it.

'You'll love it, just you and the fishes,' she said. 'You'll have company.'

At least she hadn't come right out and said it was because he lived on his own like a loser, and fishes were the nearest thing he had to friends, but she might as well have – even if she did look at him, smiling, from under those dark lashes.

Maybe, it wouldn't have been so bad if his other colleagues hadn't ribbed him about it.

'Woo-ooh mate,' Alan had called to him across the canteen. 'Mind you don't meet any ghost sharks!' Then he'd laughed like a drain so that everyone else had joined in. After that, he couldn't turn a corner without one or other of his cronies would jump out making ghost noises and baring their jaws.

'Don't worry,' Mel told him. 'They're just jealous. It's lovely at night, kind of magical. You'll see.'

It hadn't made him feel any better. The 'magic' was what he was afraid of. He reached the bottom of the ramp and stared up at the glowing water. The cod and the sardines were still swimming slowly round and round, catching the light on their scales, glowing silver like moonlight on glass. The effect was hypnotic. He closed his eyes and let the light play on his eyelids. What he wouldn't give for his bed now. He opened them again. He felt vulnerable standing there in a public space. Even with no one there to see him, it was odd behaviour. Supposing someone came in and crept up on him from behind? He whipped around. No one was there. It was just the open seating and him. There were no other noises, just the gentle lull of the bubbles.

A shadow swept past and he turned again to see the aquarium shark swim past, close to the front. Of course there wasn't a ghost. Nothing was different at night. Of course it wasn't. It was exactly the same as during the day, only darker and quieter. Martin smiled to himself. He was just being silly.

Soup in the Microwave

When Gary looked back now, he could see why she left him. It was the soup in the microwave that did it. Of course she hadn't liked the toenail clippings he left on the sofa, or the hairs in the bath, or the toilet paper down the loo, but they were the least of his sins compared to the soup.

To be honest, he thought, she'd brought it on herself. If she hadn't told him how to use the blessed thing, how was he to know that you couldn't put a can of tomato soup in there to heat up? It hadn't said anything about not putting soup in a microwave on the can either, so he supposed they were partly to blame too; but the point was, he wasn't, so when the can burst and splattered the whole thing with scalding liquid and shards of metal it was so not his fault.

Her telling him that he had to clean it up was totally unfair too. You couldn't just open a microwave that had stopped working just like that. There was the radioactivity to think about. He could get cancer, and how would she like it if he died because she made him do it? And what about those sharp shards of metal? They were contaminated too. The microwave had sat there with its covering of tomato soup, slowly going green inside because she refused to do anything about it.

Gary looked at it now and laughed. Of course it had been lucky for him. Without the microwave going bust, he might never have found Janice at the pizza parlour. Beautiful Janice, whom he got to know from his frequent visits there, looking for dinner – preferably pre-made. Of course, the best thing about Janice was watching her work. He'd watched her cleaning up at the end of the day, wiping down the ovens and swinging her long black hair. The very sound of her slapping on the marigolds with a twang gave him a shiver up his spine. Let Gloria walk out on him, Janice was moving in.

Yes, Janice was the only girl for him. She'd know what to do with the microwave.

He looked up as the shark came back and pulled a face at it. The shark made no change in its path. Its dull eyes still stared out ahead of it as it smoothed off back into the depths of the pool, disappearing into the fog of the water.

Martin snorted. He heard the muffled chime of the clock in the background, striking midnight. Of course nothing was going to happen. He walked back. Time to see how the upper level was doing. As his footsteps faded away the fish still swam round and round, as they always had. He didn't see Mel's face watching him from behind the glass, then with a swish of her tail, she was gone too.

Dorothy looked up. The wind was shooting the clouds across the sky. She knew these hills like they were another member of the family, and she knew their moods as well as her brother's. A storm was brewing.

'I think it's time to go, William,' she called to him and clutched at her bonnet.

'Not quite yet, sister dear.' William stood on the peak looking down. 'My muse is coming, I can feel it.'

Dorothy looked at the black cloud heading their way. To be caught out here in a thunderstorm and exposed to the extremes of the weather was not just foolhardy, but downright dangerous, but William liked to think he was at one with nature.

'I think it might be advisable if we were to take a slow walk along the dale, just to be on the safe side.'

William turned around, raising his eyes to the heavens. 'Very well. I think I have the first line anyway. Our walk must be completed in silence to allow me to think.'

Fine by me, thought Dorothy.

They wandered back a little slowly, allowing for William's muse, reaching the little cottage as the sky darkened. Dorothy felt pleased that the rain only started once they reached her little garden. It showed that William was getting better at doing what she told him.

'I must away to my room to write,' said William entering the hallway and making for the stairs. 'I'll take a cup of tea if you please, Dorothy.'

He didn't see Dorothy roll her eyes.

Four hours later, Dorothy had organised dinner and was now sewing up the holes in some of William's undergarments. The door opened with a bang. William emerged with his piece of paper and planted it proudly in front of her. Dorothy looked over her sewing at the multiple crossings-out and spelling mistakes and sighed.

'Do you want me to write this up for you?' she asked.

'Why thank you, sister dear.' William put a hand against his forehead. 'And now I must take to my bed for the effort has fair worn me out.'

Dorothy put the sewing down and went to sit down at her desk.

'I walked down the road and saw a cow,' William had written. No, that wouldn't do at all. She dipped her nib in the ink and made a fresh start.

'I wandered lonely as a cloud . . .'

Blurred and Slurred

'No, Jamie,' Colin said for the thousandth time. 'You can't have a milkshake.' He looked up at the heavy clouds and shivered. Shirley had been gone the whole day and from what Jamie said, several days before that too. Thank goodness the lad had the presence of mind to ring him. Perhaps he should have called the cops when he got there, but he knew where she was. Besides, he'd called them before and what good had it done? They found her, let him know and then buggered off. There was only one thing he could do.

The pavements were full of puddles, twinkling orange in the streetlights as they tramped along. Ellie sobbed at first as he took her out of the cot, but when he said they were going to see Mummy, she'd cheered up. Now she lay with her head against his chest, wrapped up inside his coat, warm and snug.

Jamie was different. He was excited, but after wandering

through the deserted shops for an hour or so, he'd started to complain.

'Why couldn't I bring my toy train?'

'Because we'd have to carry it.'

'Can we have a McDonald's?'

'No, Jamie. I haven't got any money.'

'Can I –'

'No, Jamie!'

He regretted the raised voice. Jamie lapsed into a tense silence. He was a good kid. In all the time Colin had known him, he'd never seen the boy cry.

'We've got to cross the road. Press the button.'

Jamie did as he was told. Whether he knew it was just a ruse or not, Colin didn't know. There wasn't a car in sight. They walked across holding hands. Voices could be heard now: the low mumble of chat, the occasional laugh. Colin took the kids past the window of the pub and up to the doorway. A burly man in dark glasses stood in their way.

'Sorry Sir, no children allowed in the bar.'

'I'm looking for someone,' said Colin. 'Shirley Dinton: tall woman, blonde hair. She's got a mole . . . he pointed to his cheek.

The man nodded, looked at Jamie then back at him. 'I know. I'll get her to come out to you shall I?'

'Please.'

The man looked at Jamie again, then turned and pushed his way inside. Jamie had his mother's hair and eyes. A burst of noise swept through the door then disappeared again as it swung shut.

'I'm cold,' said Jamie.

Colin patted his head. 'Not long now.'

The door was flung open. Shirley stumbled into view and stood there holding the door open. She was dressed in black, hair up but slipping down, a half-empty beer glass in her hand.

'Who are you and what d'you think you're playing at?' Her voice was slurred. He felt Ellie stir under the coat, and took a step forward.

'It's your kids, Shirley. Don't you recognise them?'

Jamie tugged her short skirt. 'Mummy, when are you coming home?'

Her eyes seemed to suddenly focus and she looked down at him.

'We're going, Shirley. We're going back to Mum's, then I'm taking them home with me. You can't just leave them for days on their own.'

She looked up at him. 'The court said they're mine, not yours. The money's mine.'

'I don't care. I'm not having them treated like this.'

Shirley glared at him and then bent down to Jamie, chucking him under the chin. 'You don't want to leave your Mum do you, sweetie?'

Jamie stood transfixed. He stared at her, eyes locked on hers, not moving. Shirley smiled. For a moment, Colin thought he was going to crack. He stretched out his hand.

'It's too late. Come on, Jamie.' Jamie shook his head as if waking from a deep dream, and loosened Shirley's grip on his face, then he turned and took Colin's hand. 'Goodbye.'

Colin began to walk away. Behind him, Shirley spluttered expletives into the night. As the rain began to fall in earnest, he heard her scream.

Caroline Davies

Love in Idleness

Prompt: Malignant tendencies

Jack Spear's hand hovers over the array of quill pens on the oak table. It's late and he must commence work. His hand swoops down – barn owl white. His choice of feather ought not to influence him, but white should produce something joyful, a play to make Will laugh.

Jack sharpens the quill with a small knife. He smoothes out the parchment but his mind refuses to settle. Today he must cover ten sheets or face Will's anger. Will's raven black quill will slash through many of the words and he'll say it isn't good enough. Jack knows this isn't true. He knows his brother as well as his own heartbeats and understands the value of his words to Will.

Will came home long after dark last night. Jack heard his stallion's whinny on reaching home. That was why Anne had not come to his bed. She knew when Will would return, seemingly by instinct. Sleeping alone meant Jack was visited by nightmares, without Anne to hold him. She would tell him he was safe but it was Will who was at risk in these dreams where Jack would plunge a knife deep into his breast. He knew that if he were to do it in real life he would have to follow his twin into the darkness of the grave. It is only this which stops him.

Chimes sound from the church tower and Jack counts to twelve. He listens for the shuffle of the maid's footsteps along the hallway and hears the clink of the bowl being set down on the flagstones outside his door. He'll wait for her to withdraw before he opens the flap to take in his luncheon. The servants have been told not to speak to him. Whenever he's tried the maid has stumbled away as if in fear of her life. Will's doing, no doubt. Only he and Anne have a key. Although Jack has often begged to be let out Will has told him it's safer. If the authorities discovered he was abroad they would surely hang him.

Jack puts down the white quill and holds up his hand. He can see the blood dripping from his fingers. He lowers his face into the sieve of his hands for a moment before starting up in horror but the fingers hold not a trace of blood. Will had dragged him to the pump in the yard and scrubbed and scrubbed until he was spotless.

Jack shudders and tries to clear his mind. Will has warned him not to dwell on these things, unless he is going to turn them into words. Jack knows this is his salvation.

Jack picks up the quill, summoning a forest at night, a group of actors, Will's friends and, unseen by them, spirits flitting through the trees. His brother will turn them into fairies, but it doesn't matter. Jack writes, as the fairies gather the flowers love-in-idleness and plot mischief amongst the mortals.

Total Immersion
(For Elizabeth Bishop)
Prompt: Open road

Reading, like travel
leads you on and on.

Both require a necessary solitude.
Travelling in company isolates you,

from the country you're in.
Silence is required

to hear the language of the poem,
the rhythm and melody.

I immerse myself in poems
like a voyager on a foreign beach.

Useless dipping toes in the brine
You have to stride until the waves

reach your waist. Cold water
shock bringing you alive.

Helen Harvey

Hunter Gatherers
Prompt: Mum's gone to Iceland

Mum has gone to Iceland,
Dad has gone to France;
Mum will bring back frozen food,
but Dad won't stand a chance –

– cos Mum has gone to Iceland
so she'll be back by three;
but Dad got on the ferry,
so he'll be late for tea.

Mum has gone to Iceland
for pizza, cakes and peas;
Dad across the channel
will get snails and sweaty cheese.

Mum has gone to Iceland
with pound coins in her purse;
Dad must pay with euros –
his bill will be much worse.

Dad tried to help with shopping
but he didn't understand:
Mum doesn't leave the country,
she just goes to Iceland.

Lie with me

Lie
with me.
Promise me
that you love me
and I'll let you stay,
let you kiss me, touch me,
spend the night with me, and I'll
promise you there are no strings attached.
Lie with me and we'll lie together.

Interpreting the data

Prompt: Tiny little feet

It happens all over the country. The evidence is there to see; you just have to understand what you're looking at.

The fiddle starts up in the darkness, playing a lively ditty that calls the dancers out. A couple of penny whistles join in, jostling in harmony around the fiddler; a drummer taps out a beat that puts sparkle into the stars.

One by one, little folk with tiny little feet in tiny stiletto heels tiptoe from their hiding places around the grassy rim and onto the makeshift dance floor. The disco moon spins.

They start to boogie, twisting and bopping, shaking the dew across the field, their miniature heels poking into the mud like a thousand notes escaped from a stave. They dance and jive and swing and sway until the night yawns and the party falls to slumber. One by one, tiny folk with tiny feet tiptoe back away, leaving little footprints dimpling the bare ground.

It happens all over the country, the evidence is plain in every goal mouth on every football pitch. It's just a case of correctly interpreting the data.

Long Days

Prompt: Alphabetical order

The letters are set out in alphabetical order. On better days, Mary points to spell T-E-A or L-O-V-E or whatever she needs or still has to give, though it might choke her.

On bad days, Ellie has to point for her, one letter after another. Mary holds her daughter's hand and squeezes when she reaches the right letter. It achieves the same, though it's tediously drawn out. Each letter might be an hour, a day; so it feels.

Most days, Mary only blinks slowly from one letter to the next. Her eyes say it all.

Olivia Bell

Forget all I want to Remember

Prompt: Secret Letters

There in my cupboard
lies a box,
a box with too many memories
for me to memorise.
So I kept a box to simply
remember all I'd forget,
but sometimes,
just sometimes, I wish that
box would disappear, so I could
forget my mistakes,
forget the past and all I never
did, all I wanted but
was too scared to seize,
to hold onto tightly, through
anything.
There, in my box lie
the secrets of my past,
the love I was sent
and the love I threw away.
So just sometimes,
when it's a black day
I wish I could forget
all I wanted to remember.

Lost In Thoughts
Prompt: Give me a break!

Music switched on,
turned up and up and up,
drowning out thoughts and sounds,
scribbling down
streams of thoughts.
Music stops dead,
a strange, strained silence,
eyes reopened,
left wondering what all
the scribble on the page means,
where it came from and
what inspired it.
She is
lost.

Left to pick up the Pieces

Prompt: Grandpa's chair

Lowered into the ground,
left to rest in peace,
forget the troubling
past years,
moving on, leaving us
behind.
Slowly we walk away,
back to the cottage,
we look and stare at
the reminders of everything
you left behind.
It looks just like you left to go shopping,
instead we know you won't
return to create more mess,
we are left alone,
left to pick up the pieces.
You were different,
forgetting silly little things
and then it got bad and
you began to
forget me.
And I miss you
and everything I could
have had,
I miss what could have been
and I'm left sitting here
looking at my surroundings
wondering how God
could bestow such
sorrow upon us.

Stare Future in the Eyes
Prompts: In the back row / Don't look back

Tapping their feet to the beat,
swaying in the moment,
enjoying the odd
unpredictable tune.
Five, six, seven eight,
they begin their dance,
quick,
slow,
slow,
quick, quick,
slow.
Stop!
Five, six, seven, eight,
slow, quick, slow, slow,
head held up high,
eyes forward,
focus on the present
the future
don't look behind
don't look at the people in
the back row,
the ones that mess up,
the ones that can't look forward,
don't look back
it won't help,
look forward,
stare the future in the eye.

Fading Memories

Prompt: A Photograph of Her

Memories fade despite
your wish for it to be
fresh and new,
wishing and wanting
sometimes isn't enough,
memories fade, I find
your image no longer as
vivid in my mind,
I see you only just,
I'm forced to stare
at pictures of you
to simply remind myself,
to refresh my memory,
that you were once real.
And try as I might
I cannot help but feel
a failure, for forgetting
your beautiful smile.

Pull Me In

Prompt: Quicksand

Like quicksand you're
pulling me in,
tempting me,
calling me.
I can't help but
lose myself in your chase,
let go,
forget common sense,
another day and it'll be
over,
too late and I'll be
lost.
So I'll let go and
fall with you,
let myself be sucked in,
taken and forget to
fight for freedom,
freedom lies anyway
with you.

Sleepless Night

Prompt: Another sleepless night

Here we are again,
it's two a.m.,
another night spent
talking
rather than dreaming.
Keeping one another
up, while the moon falls,
the sun rises, and slowly
conversation quietens as
we prepare for an end to our
dreamless, sleepless night.
Spend the day on
automatic,
day dreaming, yawning,
waiting for another night
where we are alone.

Waiting for a Beginning

Prompt: When will it begin?

Day in and day out
I try not to wait,
I move forward
focusing on each step,
each moment, each breath,
but I can't help but
wonder when we'll begin.

Hywela Lyn

Count Your Blessings

Prompt: The Curse

Thomas thrust his hands deep into his pockets and averted his eyes as he approached the heap of rags huddled in the doorway. A gnarled, withered hand reached out to him and he shrank away with a shudder.

Beggars! Ought to be rounded up, the lot of 'em. Rounded up and made to do a decent day's work. It should be illegal – come to think of it, it already was, wasn't it? He would check when he arrived home. There must be something on the internet about beggars and what could be done about them.

'Can you spare a pound coin for a san'wich an' a cuppa tea, kind sir?'

The words, barely audible, were almost lost in a paroxysm of coughing. Thomas turned away and lashed out with his gleaming city shoe. There was a muffled cry and a plastic plate rattled across the pavement, the few coins it contained rolling across the dusty concrete. He glimpsed the old crone scrabbling desperately on her hands and knees, before she was lost in the milling crowds of shoppers. He heard a voice in his mind:

Curse you. May you be cursed from this day forward.

He pursed his lips. His mind was playing tricks. He'd been working too hard. Anyway, even if it wasn't his imagination, he wasn't going to let the words of a hideous old beggar worry him. He glanced at his watch. If he hurried he'd be able to put in a round of golf. Lord knew he worked hard enough. He'd intended to spend his one free afternoon a week doing his accounts, but why not relax with a round or two? After all, it was a beautiful day . . .

. . . three holes in one. Thomas grinned broadly. So much

for curses. He'd never had this happen before. Once more he addressed the ball. He could hardly believe his luck. By the time it happened for the tenth time, he realised perhaps things were not quite as they seemed.

He looked around. It seemed he was alone on the golf course, which stretched endlessly ahead of him. The sky, which had been so bright and clear earlier was now leaden and grey, although the heat was stiffing. Again and again he swung his club, and each time was result was the same.

In the back of his mind he heard a maniacal chuckle. The realisation hit him then that he was never going home.

Grandpa's Chair

The funeral was over, the Will had been read. Tamzin tried to hide her disappointment. After all, she had not really expected Grandpa to leave her anything, although a few thousand pounds would have been very useful at the moment, with the kids starting school and the landlord putting up the rent. Still, the old rocking chair had been her grandpa's favourite. She could remember sitting on it she was a little girl. Of his five grandchildren, she had spent the most time with him. Even when she grew up and married and had children of her own, she had visited him as often as she could.

He used to say she was the only one of his grandchildren who cared about him, but she was sure that was not true. If it was, why did he leave each of the others five thousand pounds? He must have loved them and believed they loved him as much. Their father, Grandpa's only son, died a few years ago and their mother left home when Tamzin was a teenager.

She smiled to herself. After all, he had left her his favourite chair, a chair of memories. Nothing could be more precious than that.

'But what about the house?' That was Sarah, her younger sister. 'There's no mention of the house in the Will. Well, the old codger was well into his nineties, I suppose he forgot about it. It'll have to be sold and the money shared out –' The other three siblings nodded in agreement. Tamzin could almost see the pound signs in their eyes. She hated the thought of the lovely, rambling old house being sold to strangers.

Tom, Tamzin's husband, put a gentle hand around his wife's shoulder and glared at Sarah. 'I think you ought to see a solicitor to check on that –'

'Who asked you?' Sarah spat out and turned back to the others.

'Leave them to it, Luv,' Tom said, seeing the tears in Tamzin's eyes. 'Come on, let's get this old rocking chair into the van and go home.'

Later that evening as they sat in front of the fire, the children tucked up safely in bed, Tom gave his wife a hug.

'I'll make us a nice cup of cocoa, shall I Luv? I know how fond you were of your granddad, it's been a hard day for you. And those hard nosed sisters and brother of yours should be ashamed they way the acted.'

As her husband busied himself in the kitchen, Tamzin leaned back in the chair and rocked gently back and fro. She wriggled a bit, wondering why it felt so uncomfortable. At last she jumped up and shook the cushion vigorously, trying to plump it up. Something fell out onto the floor. She picked it up and examined it curiously. A large brown envelope – and inside what looked like a legal document – and a note.

'My dearest Tamzin,' she read. 'Of all my grandchildren you were the only one who really cared about me. I have instructed my solicitor to make over the title deeds of my house to you and Tom by Deed of Gift. I knew if I left it

to you in my Will the others would contest it. I've seen you and Tom struggle over the past few years and I've made sure at least you will have a decent roof over your heads to call your own.
All my love, Grandpa.'

Walking with Wordsworth

'And all at once I saw a host, a crowd of golden daffodils.'

I walk through the trees, the lines of poetry running through my head. As far as I can see, the beautiful yellow flowers stretch into the distance each side of me and straight ahead, covering the banks of the river, nodding their heads in the light wind, just like in the poem.

On and on I walk, listening to the birdsong and revelling in the tranquillity and beauty all around me. I think about the long-dead poet, whose spirits were lifted by his memories of the daffodils. I watch the dragonflies skim above the water, and marvel.

Where did we go wrong? If only life could be as simple as it was when Wordsworth was alive. I take one last look at the daffodils, 'nodding and dancing in the breeze.'

With a sigh I turn and leave the room. As the door hums closed, I touch a button to shut down the hologram and gaze in despair through the opaque sides of the dome, at a dead and barren Earth. A world which will never again, thanks to the ignorance of mankind, see the beauty of real, living daffodils.